To
RUBY TURBERVILLE
and
'RUSTY'
(who is herself)
with love

f4.95

3
)

The White Rose

ALANNA KNIGHT

The White Rose

HURST & BLACKETT

HURST & BLACKETT LTD
3 Fitzroy Square, London W1

AN IMPRINT OF THE HUTCHINSON GROUP

London Melbourne Sydney Auckland
Wellington Johannesburg Cape Town
and agencies throughout the world

First published 1973

*This book has been set in Baskerville type, printed in Great Britain
on antique wove paper by Anchor Press, and
bound by Wm. Brendon, both of Tiptree, Essex*

ISBN 0 09 117420 1

I

Lamb-white springtime blossomed over a countryside suspiciously resembling a Landseer reproduction. The Highland scene beloved of dark halls in third-rate guest houses lacked only the Monarch of the Glen, the Stag at Bay, brooding in the middle distance.

As compensation, however, there brooded along the village street a red-headed young man in kilt and shaggy Aran sweater, Scots as porridge oats, his countenance all planes and angles. It was the kind of face that conjures up Scotland's lost heroes, William Wallace and Robert the Bruce, and long before them the warrior Vikings from across the cold North Sea. Above features of such strength, bright red curls were an ill-set frivolity and quite put to shame the modest auburn locks of the Irish setter walking gracefully at his side.

Both man and beast had fine noble heads, and airs of good breeding. The dog won on mere points of elegance. They were such a delightful addition to an already perfect scene that I could have leaped out of the bus and embraced them both—just for being there. As they walked purposefully down the street, out of sight and out of my life, I felt strangely bereft in a world made emptier by their passing. If only I could have known something more about them . . .

As the bus moved off again, I decided I had been wrong about my landscape. In two days I had discovered a tougher country than one hitherto associated with bagpipes, jokes about haggis, Tartan Unlimited, and kilted comedians. Beautiful this country was, but unsentimental. Breath-taking grandeur, the feeling that none of it was quite real, concealed a certain inflexibility, an indomitable endurance and pride. Here one did battle constantly for survival—and sometimes lost. The past I had identified, momentarily and whimsically, with the young man with red hair was everywhere in these wild hills.

Even the seasons made their own rules and I suspected took their own vengeance. I had shivered since arrival in small hotels where I was painstakingly informed that the 'tourist season' had not yet started. Where slipping between pristine white linen sheets each night was more like drowning in the ice-cold loch outside the windows than comfortably retiring to bed. Despite a calendar which pointed to late spring, here winter still reigned—at that moment personified by a sudden dark cloud and accompanying flurry of enormous hailstones.

I sighed. How Ben would have loved the drama of it all. As was my custom when we were apart, I described it to him in one of those interminable monologues inside my head which, when he was abroad, erupted in carefully worded letters, spiced with witty observations. These were gleaned almost entirely from his prescribed reading list for me during his undergraduate days, when I had entered his family as his mother's secretary.

With formal education limited to the expensive local girls' school, the Armstrongs considered my ignorance at sixteen appalling. To Rona and Ben I soon learned that brains were revered only a little less than money. However, with parrot-like expertise and willingness to learn, in a relatively short time I talked 'Ben's language' and the criterion of my hero-worship became a judgement of all behaviour and attitudes, my own and everyone else's, as to whether Ben present or absent would approve, whether they would bring a smile of approval or a frown of displeasure to his handsome face.

The landscape rolled by, taking with it a tear that rolled down my cheek. For there was no Ben to talk to in my head or anywhere else any more. At least, not for me. He no longer sat enthroned in imagination, smile or frown at the ready. Ben, fiancé of the past five years, was going to marry someone else much more suited by academic qualification—and money—than myself.

Rona, his mother, had sent me on this wild-goose chase to the Highlands to look over a summer cottage she saw advertised in *The Times*. 'It might have possibilities for summer holidays, you know,' she had enthused, going on rather too long about : 'my need to emerge from air pollution and Perseus Plastics Ltd. once or twice a year, and to breathe decent honest air again.'

Dear Rona, who flew to Marrakesh or Portugal to roast in the sun each spring, to whom the damp and downpours of the Scottish Highland summer would be intolerable. It was an innocent deception and I forgave her, torn as she was between Ben, flesh of her flesh, bone of her bone, and the girl she had 'brought up by hand' after my father, the senior partner in Perseus Plastics, died of a heart attack.

There had never been a moment's doubt or hesitation in Rona's mind that I should go to Aynley House. After that it had all seemed so right and natural that Ben and I should fall in love, for I had adored him since the days when Rona, a young widow, joined the firm as junior partner. While she went to conferences abroad, Ben had been left with my father and me and our succession of efficient, emotionless housekeepers who took the place of the mother who had died when I was two.

Pretending small girl's sex-hatred and contempt of boys was impossible with Ben. Even as a child he commanded respect. Never knobbly-kneed, acned or gauche, he was born elegant, with a dark lean face like a Pharaoh straight from an Egyptian tomb and long slim hands. When I went to live with them he had been graduated from Cambridge for two years and was working in the firm.

'Business administration experience is invaluable,' Rona had said and eyeing me soulfully, for she had never been known to let a bargain slip her grasp: 'I do need a secretary, someone efficient and reliable—a girl I can trust.' Later she had remarked: 'There was no point in sending you to university, even had you wanted to go. It was obvious to everyone that you would marry Ben in a year or two.'

During those years Ben acquired more polish and experience on trips abroad, plus a long list of name-droppable friends who had yachts in the Mediterranean, while Rona and I roosted in the factory, two uneasy hens in a nightmare nest of coloured plastics.

Perhaps I should have sensed the wind of change was blowing had pride allowed me the luxury of ruthless honesty. While Ben explored and expanded his horizons, I remained at home, warming his slippers, content to look on our wedding day which remained obstinately in the future, ephemeral as a desert mirage. It was always: 'Another six months, darling. You're too young, Candida, my pet.' And Ben would ruffle my hair and return me firmly to the little-sister image he loved. When he returned from New York two months ago there was a lot of urgent private chat late at night with his mother. From their guilty agonised looks when I entered a room unexpectedly I suspected some financial crisis they were keeping from me. But in due course Ben painfully informed me that the much-needed fund-raising trip had been wildly successful. In fact, his latest take-over bid also included his rich rival's daughter and a splended dowry.

I thought he was joking. Knowing how much the firm meant to Ben and Rona, I was prepared to make reasonable allowances and in the shock that I'm told makes a soldier who loses a leg in battle still 'feel' his foot I told myself on sleepless nights that it was only Debbie's money that mattered. Ben could never tire of me, nor outgrow our wonderful years together. In some way our love would remain and he would return to me in the end. With my enormous capacity for daydreams, boosted by sudden morbid interest in horoscopes and amateur tea-cup astrology, I saw him at the end of a long corridor of time, taking me until death us do part—his own true love in a flurry of wedding bells. If only I couldn't remember his solemn words that sounded the death-knell to our love :

'It will be best for you, too, Candida. You'll be glad some day, you'll see. After all, aren't we more like brother and sister than lovers should be?'

We had never been lovers. Perhaps that was what was wrong, I thought fiercely and too late, my tearful offering of *anything* for him was received with a sweet smile, a gentle kiss and : 'Silly girl, that wouldn't make the slightest difference. I shall always love you, like a brother. Some day you'll meet a man who'll appreciate you. . . .'

If I had needed words to tell me it was truly all over, now I had heard them, remembering Ben, jealous, possessive, capable of making the most terrible scenes if I so much as looked at another boy. Older by six years, wiser in worldly experience, so protective I sometimes felt smothered. Now free for the first time in my adult life, I felt nothing kindly as relief, only an increasing awareness as day folded into week and week into month, and Debbie from Dallas, Texas, became a reality to be reckoned with, that Ben had gone and with him some vital part of the intricate mechanism by which I had my being. A dull empty physical ache, a hunger in the heart that could never be appeased. . . .

A sign flashed by outside the bus. Muldoune Bridge. Towering mountains, fir trees and a great torrent of water over a dark ravine. We stopped by the window of a woollen mill. 'Hand-made tweeds. Visitors welcome.' There was a tantalising glimpse of delicate muted shades of blues, purples, greens, pinks, all strangely at ease as if they had been distilled in some magical way from the background.

And there in the centre of the window was a sweater. I blinked. A man's sweater that had surely been made in heaven for Ben. I saw him wearing it, his favourite colour and style—and I saw him loving me anew for such a gift.

Assured by the driver of a ten-minute wait, I leaped into the shop, wading through that sea of colour. Sweaters, cardigans, skirts, coats, bales of rainbow tweeds and silken mohairs. Kilts, tartan ties and cash-mere sweaters.

And there was Ben's. The size was right, only the price brought momentary misgivings. It would leave me nothing but my return ticket to York. I hesitated, then decided as this bus took me to Aberdeen, where

I joined the train home, I didn't need money. Besides, Ben was worth every pound. So carrying sweater in one hand and wallet in the other, I trailed the only assistant at the heels of a large vociferous woman bullying her nervous husband into the choice of a tartan tie. Keeping a wary eye on the stationary bus, I lingered in their wake tactfully examining sealskin purses and wishing I had enough money left to take one back for Rona.

At last I had the shop to myself and handing over my purchase was unable to resist a further delay for the vanity of a luxurious box. Ben set great store on the finer touches, for him the elegant wrappings in life were secondary only to the contents. Waiting, I took another regretful look at the purses and reached the bus just as it was moving.

The conductress shrugged at my apology, indicating that this was a regular occurrence. Clutching my parcel, well pleased with its extravagance, the magnificent countryside passed unseen for a while as imagination lingered over a naively tender scene in which Ben, taking out the sweater, was stricken by remorse, and confided that he suspected Debbie was rather mean. . . .

'Tickets, please.' Opening handbag for wallet, my blood literally ran to ice. Heart hammering, I spilled out the shamefully untidy contents on to my lap. Make-up, comb, letters, book-matches which I never used, carried for the Perseus Plastics insignia—a purse, empty but for a few coins . . . The missing wallet containing bus ticket and rail ticket to York was reposing among the sealskin purses back in the woollen mill.

'I've left it—I'll have to go back—I'm sorry.' As I gabbled an explanation, I felt sure the conductress's suspicious glance suggested that she was considering dumping me into that unrealistic but beautiful scenery whipping past the windows, as the bus sped further away from Muldoune Bridge.

The driver who had stopped to take up passengers heard it all and consulting his watch said: 'If you look sharp you can catch the bus back to Muldoune there, across the road. Don't worry, lass, if the shop is closed, the Macauleys live in the house attached to the mill.'

I was just in time and five minutes later I had spent my last precious pence on a ticket back to Muldoune Bridge. Alas, the shop was closed, the door locked. But worse was to come. I rang the house doorbell repeatedly and, sure it didn't work, in desperation began an anxious investigation of the house by a side path. A few moments later I was uncomfortably aware of a small van bearing 'Police' in large letters on its brow and three suspiciously alert pairs of eyes studying my behaviour with considerable interest.

As I stammered out my predicament, they beamed. Obviously delighted at the prospect of a little action, they suggested I walk across the road to the station and tell my story there.

Television serials had been my only experience of policemen until then and I was content for my arm-chair view to remain the only contact. Feeling criminal in every pore as I repeated my story, I realised that the expertise of television policemen bore no resemblance to the inside of a remote Highland bastion of the law.

As I described the disaster to a yawning, unsmiling lawman with exact contents, colour, etc., of the wallet, plus time of loss, he dragged out an enormous official form and with some difficulty produced a ball-point-pen that worked.

'Your full name please?'

'Candida Deveron Brent.'

The spelling of Candida halted him for a while, so did my Yorkshire address. This obstacle removed, my date and place of birth were easy, and we went from strength to strength with mother's maiden name, father's name and occupation, their date of marriage, etc., so that I had distinct visions of Holloway Prison as my next forwarding address, and trembled to think of details I would have had to supply had I committed a real crime like petty larceny.

Eventually one of the trio from Muldoune's 'Z Cars' came out with a tray: 'Here you are, lass, might as well have a cup o' tea. I've been making enquiries and Macauley and his wife are awa' to the airport, flying over to Paris for the spring weekend. That was your last bus to Aberdeen, it's a long wait you'll be having here—until Tuesday when the shop opens again.'

With no cheque book, no money, I was considering what vagrancy would make me eligible for free board and lodgings behind bars when on the map behind the desk the name 'Deveron' caught my eye.

Deveron. And I remembered Great-Uncle Fraser Deveron.

'Beg pardon, miss.'

I repeated his name and the policeman looked vastly relieved.

'It's only thirty miles away,' said the tea-maker called Sandy, snatching up the phone book. He thumbed through triumphantly, then said: 'He's no' listed here.'

'He's elderly, a bachelor—and rather eccentric.'

Sandy scratched his cheek. 'A castle, you say? Ah well.' And they exchanged glances which I interpreted as a laird vague and impoverished and not to be trachled with things modern.

'Fraser Deveron, did you say? Now I thought he died, oh, ten years back and left a laddie as heir.'

'Can't be the same man. He visited us in Yorkshire five years ago.'

Sandy frowned, shaking his head. 'I was sure . . .'

'Ah, man,' said the form-filler, 'there's a great clan of Deverons, the lassie should know.'

'Tell me how I get to Deveron Castle.'

There was no direct transport service. Deveron could only be reached by changing buses twice. 'The Aberdeen bus would have taken you part of the way, but there isn't another today.'

Sandy snapped his fingers. 'Got it. There's one of yon pop groups playing at a Ceilidh which will be passing through Deveron village on its way,' he yelled and rushed to the door. 'There he is now,' Sandy flagged down the driver, who was obviously the possessor of many guilty secrets if his haunted countenance could be believed. Sandy had given him the fright of his life and when he realised it was just another passenger and not a search of the musical instuments he was so delighted he would have taken me to the moon had I wished.

Once inside the mini-bus, I found my companions a silent group, gloomy too, and suspected there were matters of some illegality afoot, or, more correctly, abus, perhaps cannabis stacked inside fiddles and guitars. Certainly when Deveron appeared they set me down hurriedly and, turning me in the right direction, departed with promptitude and evident relief. Perhaps they thought I was a policewoman in disguise, but I'll never know.

'Glen Deveron, ½m.', wheedled the signpost, and I

started down the road walked by my maternal ancestors, feeling distinctly apprehensive and very cold.

'In Scotland we have weather not climate.' I remembered Great-Uncle Fraser's words, obviously uttered from the heart. The road before me was arched by tall trees where at least the rooks were in no doubt of the season. The still bare trees bloomed with dark round shapes of nests, while enormous black bird shapes screamed raucously above my head.

It was like a scene from a horror film, birds of ill-omen. One flopped down and settled on the fence, waddling along beside me, like a shabby old gent in evening dress, keeping pace and eyeing me with malevolence, to be joined by one, then two, then three. They descended gracelessly from the trees, and I felt there was something remarkably predatory in their united watchful gaze.

It was idiotic, but I wanted to take to my heels. Birds of ill-omen, ill-omen, echoed my now hurrying footsteps.

At last the lane had its turning and there across the field was a towering mountain, Cairn Dever, and the loch that Great-Uncle Fraser had described, plus a castle which even at this distance looked worn-out, perhaps by its struggles to keep up with the passing centuries. Its windows were narrow and looked rather cross-eyed with the stern watching, no doubt, of the modern world and the tourist traffic that, by evidence of litter baskets prominently displayed, streamed along the river bank on warmer days than this.

Heartened by the appearance of my destination, I began composing a conversation with Ben and Rona about my adventures. How Ben would love it—how he would laugh. And then I stopped. The rooks were gone, all was silent around me.

It was as if I had stopped to hear Ben's laugh. No, he wouldn't laugh, not for me any more. And I wondered sadly, as I died a little more inside, how long I would go on before I could shed Ben's image as part of my living and breathing, my whole existence. Faced with the prospect of parting company with Ben, Rona, the home I shared with them, my own little office in Perseus Plastics, I suddenly realised that all I had left in the world as kin was the eccentric old man who lived in the castle across the field there.

The glimpse of castle vanished behind high estate walls and I walked hopefully, expecting it eventually to disgorge lodge gates. After ten minutes of brisk walking I paused and looked around, realising I had lost all sense of direction in the winding road, the wall and the trees. Now I wished I had been able to give Great-Uncle Fraser more notice of my arrival than a promise from the Muldoune Bridge Police to 'see if we can get a message to him that you're on your way'.

I now had a long fairly straight road to myself, shared by a fierce wind blowing flakes of snow into my face. The cold was increasing every moment and I thought with longing of the inside of the castle, the great hall with its log fire, the servants waiting on the table, the horses pawing impatiently in the stables.

'Come any time, m'dear, just give me enough notice to have the servants air the west wing for you and the factor to bring down a brace of game birds. A mere bachelor, y'know, doesn't need much, but there's a four-poster waiting for you—Mary, Queen of Scots slept in it once upon a time . . .'

But five years ago I was too absorbed with Ben and holidays in Paris, Rome or the villa in Majorca and I little thought that I would ever be tempted to the far north-east coast—'the cold shoulder of Scotland', as someone aptly described it.

But the wheel had turned and left me without a choice. And I should be grateful for my good fortune in having at least a great-uncle left in the shattered debris of my life. An optimistic imagination raced ahead—who knows, it whispered, where this day might lead? I saw myself hostessing his bachelor establishment, his shooting parties in the summer—though how I would deal with the corpses of birds or reconcile myself to their slayers I didn't stop to ponder. Then looking up at the mountain I decided there would be ski-ing in winter and, who knows, a handsome visitor who might make me forget Ben.

Perhaps one day I would decide I had been lucky meeting Great-Uncle Fraser, for few people owed their good fortune to a more slender chance of fate. During the week after my sixteenth birthday and the announcement of my engagement to Ben, Rona and I drove home to Aynley House, a large Edwardian pseudo-Tudor mansion, where Ben, lurking in the hall, ushered us mysteriously towards the lounge, with :

'There's an old gentleman to see you. Now don't laugh . . .'

Rona and I exchanged glances, expecting one of the firm's clients, until a dazzling figure resplendent in tartan stood up to greet us. He doffed a bonnet of immense proportions and bobbed a head of flowing white hair, beard and matching mustachios.

'Fine house you have here, splendid, splendid. Ah, my dear Marie,' this to Rona, 'I remember you stayed at the castle with us when you were a wee bairn.' Seizing Rona, he planted a smacking kiss on her cheek, and again, with that sweep of the bonnet, he bowed. 'Fraser Deveron, ma'am, at your service.' And turning to me he beamed. 'You must be Candida. How like your mother you are—a credit to you, ma'am.' He bobbed in Rona's direction. 'Glad to see you inherited the Deveron taste and style, m'dear,' he added, eyeing Rona's antiques, her silver on display, all of which I personally deplored as a little too ostentatious a display of sudden wealth. . . .

Rona was explaining that she wasn't Marie, my mother who had died so long ago. Fraser sighed, looked solemn and, placing bonnet over heart, raised his eyes to heaven : 'God rest her sweet soul.' And not one whit put out, he continued : 'So you have brought up my little great-niece.' He eyed me approvingly. 'And a magnificent job you have made of her.'

Ben, who, for once, had only a walking-on part, discreetly brought another whisky. Great-Uncle sank on to the settee and patted it, indicating that I should sit beside him. Then from the sporran's depths, and a thick wallet which appeared to be stuffed with a roll of banknotes firmly anchored inside an elastic band, he produced a news cutting. Smoothing it out, he said :

'Merest chance brought me here. Merest chance. Over breakfast at the Savoy, y'know, name caught my eye. Been in Paris for a reunion of the Clan Deveron and there was the name : Candida Deveron Brent, Aynley House, Aynley, Yorkshire . . .'

By the time we had it all sorted out, the old gentleman was on his third whisky and waxing poetic about the glories of Deveron and hadn't my mother told me of the grand holidays she had had at the castle, the time she fell in the loch, her adventures with the White Rose of Deveron? 'Our family ghost, y'know.'

I nodded vaguely, not wanting to upset him, for he

seemed to have forgotten completely that she had died when I was two.

Ben and Rona egged him on with his stories. Rona begged him to stay. I could see she was enchanted. Collecting eccentric characters was her second favourite hobby after antiques. Often both pastimes turned out to be exceedingly expensive, for Rona, swayed by the surface veneer, had her fair share of fakes.

Ben was watching us with his usual charming smile. He had said little, but behind that smiling interested countenance I knew he was studying Great-Uncle Fraser with the shrewdness and calculation that kept Perseus Plastics going despite his giddy adorable mother. Ben wasn't the Boss for nothing and by the time the old gentleman had left—two weeks later—I felt that Ben was a very mystified man. Once when we discussed him he said : 'A charming charlatan—but don't tell Rona.'

What if Ben had been right? Was I being absolutely mad coming on a journey like this alone? The solitude was unnerving, used as I was to a land where the sky was for ever darkened by factory chimneys, jet planes, multi-storeyed flats. I looked back down the road, deepening in evening gloom. Even the rooks had gone to bed.

What should I do? While I hesitated, a Land-Rover appeared. I waved wildly as it whizzed by. It travelled a few yards, reversed and a man with the second reddest hair I had ever seen poked his head out.

'Trouble?' he asked. He must have had the gift of prophecy for that was the beginning.

2

'Which way to Deveron?' I asked.

He opened the door. 'Jump in and I'll take you there, if you don't mind a detour. I have a call to make first.'

As we started off and I thanked him, he nodded, as if his thoughts were elsewhere, and I thought how Ben would have donned an air of authority and announced that his destination was Deveron Castle, his business with the laird. However, the driver's pre-occupation seemed to exclude curiosity.

At second glance I was almost certain this was the same man I had seen from the bus window just before my disaster at Muldoune Bridge. Even *sans* dog and considerably less elegant in jeans and anorak, it seemed unlikely that I should have encountered two people with such a strong resemblance and such striking red hair within forty miles of each other. If he had been friendlier, the fact that I had seen him earlier with his dog would have made a good ice-breaker. Even un-friendly people warm to compliments about their dogs.

There was a great deal of clattering in the back of the jeep where my case and Ben's sweater, in a box now sadly battered, reposed among a quaint assort-ment of gear—as if he had burgled Steptoe & Son's yard or was on a trading stamps bonanza. Fishing tackle, a grandfather clock which made protesting noises—nor did I blame it—a broken-down chair, mattress, oil-lamp and a fearsome shiny axe, still with price label attached. Even had my companion been less taciturn, normal conversation would have been an impossibility. Any kind of words other than those roared at the top of one's voice, and repeated three times, were quite out of the question.

'Silencer's broken and gear's stuck in second. Hang on,' he added, and that seemed an idea not without merit as we left the main road and turned on to a track climbing steeply into the hills. I had not realised human bones did rattle until then, an unenviable experience accompanied by the noisy exhaust and the full vibration of well-worn gears.

Soon there was another problem. Were my eyes growing dim with weariness, for the bright landscape was fading rapidly? I blinked. Nothing wrong with my eyes, so clinging to my seat I looked back and discovered we were enmeshed in a cotton-wool world solidly grey. All evidence of field, farm and river had disappeared as we hung noisily suspended between heaven and earth, on what was obviously the steep side of Cairn Dever, the mountain that had so impressed me by its grandeur—from the safe and solid terrain far below.

Ahead all visibility deteriorated by the second and the only indication of steepness of ascent was given by the increase of protesting noises from the engine. Once we stalled, began to slip backwards. My shriek of alarm was rewarded by a curse from the driver.

'She'll make it. Don't panic,' he said. 'Nothing's going to happen to you.'

Now that he had mentioned it, my scalp prickled with alarm. Here I was shrouded in deepest mist on a lonely mountainside with a strange sullen man who had picked me up on the roadside. Nervously I glanced back over my shoulder at the bric-à-brac, in particular that gleaming axe. My throat constricted with terror as I remembered with frightening clarity a newspaper account of a recent murder in this area

23

which I might well have considered an apt cautionary tale befitting my own predicament.

'Girl found dead on Mountain. Lonely Hitch-hiker Murdered . . .'

The driver was certainly a little crazy and, on the evidence of the axe, possibly homicidal. No, it was I who on second thoughts must be crazy. What on earth possessed me to do something in these remote wild lands that I would never once have contemplated in the noisy bustling Yorkshire town where I had spent all my life! Why had I not remembered that constant warning from my earliest days? :

Never take lifts from a stranger . . .

I tried to speak and thought I was going to say : 'Surely this isn't the right direction for Deveron?' and found instead that I was politely remarking, as the driver paused to scowl at me : 'The mist is getting thicker.'

'Um?' He looked at me directly for the first time and his eyes were clear bright blue, like polished stones under that carrot red hair.

'I said the mist's getting thicker.' I tried a faint imitation of a smile. 'I hope you know the way.'

He nodded vigorously. 'Don't worry. I'll get you to Deveron. If the worst comes to the worst we can shelter in the ski-hut until it lifts.'

Encouraged by what was quite a speech, I asked : 'How long does it usually last?'

'A few hours at this time of the year—rarely more than twelve. It's the meeting of the warm and cold air currents. I expect it'll be clear by morning.'

By morning, eh? Surely he didn't expect me to spend the night in a ski-hut with him. But that was what he had in mind. As if he read my thoughts, he said : 'Don't worry, the ski-hut is comfortable enough.

24

Better than spending a night in the open. We're used to such emergencies. Ah, there it is now.'

The appearance of a primitive-looking log cabin was about as reassuring and appealing as the Witch's House in *Hansel and Gretel.* And I feared for the same sinister reasons. Once inside and the door closed, I would be this man's prisoner, at his mercy.

I decided I was going to need all my wits to extract me from this situation into which I had heedlessly leaped. Then I noticed with secret delight that I had won an unexpected advantage in Round One, for he left the keys in the car.

The ski-hut consisted of one large room, part kitchen, part dormitory, for whatever space was not occupied by shelves and cooking utensils was occupied by bunks. The door was unlocked. Presumably only inaccessibility kept those shelves with their tins and cartons intact.

The young man watched the weather moodily for a moment. 'Sorry we're non-electric,' he said, indicating a lamp on the table. 'We're still on oil and gathering winter fuel for fires. However, it makes a pleasant change to the grosser fleshpots of civilisation,' he added, in the manner of one who expects an argument. 'Just make yourself at home while I go and get something to start a fire. Then I'll unload the car.'

A reason for the junkyard raid became apparent as furniture. 'We might as well be cosy. Choose your bed, they're all reasonably comfortable,' and he flashed a warm smile at me quite in contrast to those cold bright eyes.

I smiled in return, but the moment his footsteps died away I was out of that hut, galloping to where he had parked the car, luckily with its nose pointing downhill. Jumping into the driver's seat, I prayed silently and the engine started at the first touch of the self-starter. I wasn't a moment too soon, for the noisy blast-off brought him from the mist, leaping at me like a bat out of hell. Red hair ablaze, face contorted with rage against that grey backdrop, I didn't need to hear the words to guess they gave me a quick character reading and for good measure threw in another for my immediate ancestors.

The car jumping, bouncing like a wild steer, gears crashing, I shot out of sight down that track of road between the grass verges, travelling on what had apparently been an ancient river bed, judging by the number of stones whirring under the wheels. Suddenly the track curved upwards in a bend I didn't remember from our journey. The engine stalled, stopped and the self-starter, used to a kinder more knowledgeable hand than mine, gave a grudging hiccup and lapsed into silence.

I thrust out my head and listened. Footsteps were approaching, heavy and angry, sliding along the path. As I took to my heels, I made another discovery which lent wings to my departure: the gleaming axe was conspicuous by its absence. On I raced, following the upward path, praying that the mist was ready to oblige with a hiding-place. But only a few yards of grass were clearly visible, nibbled clean down to the roots, a few stones that wouldn't have hidden a corpulent sparrow, while the anxious bleating from behind the curtains of mist announced that I was on my own, in sheep country.

I stumbled on, refusing to be beaten, determined to reach Deveron now, even if I had to get there on hands and knees. At that moment I had little choice, anything would be better than facing this latter-day Robert the Bruce suitably armed with axe.

I looked with distaste at my weekend case and Ben's sweater, reluctant to discard one or both. Luckily, they weren't bulky enough to seriously handicap my flight. The elegant box had already suffered from exposure and I shook it angrily, the cause of all my present difficulties. If only I hadn't stopped to buy this sweater for Ben, I would have been safely on the train to York. And, giving it another shake, I fastened the string over my wrist and headed in what I hoped was the general direction of the lower reaches of the hill where there might presumably be trees to provide shelter and safety from my pursuer.

It took ten minutes and not a severe exercise of my always ready imagination to realise that both my plight and the mist had steadily worsened and somehow I had taken the wrong direction. I was now completely lost. By the time I had fallen twice, the second time nicely squashing the box containing the sweater under me, I realised that stumbling about had its own dangers. Wondering what Ben would have done, for he had a ready answer to most of life's emergencies, I decided despite discomfort that the sensible thing was to sit down, cold, soaked and hungry, and wait until the mist lifted. I hoped as I did so that my pursuer was similarly employed and that the mist would eventually lift on him in a different part of the mountain we both shared at that moment.

After twenty-one years of streets, factory chimneys, skyscrapers, towns, motorways, pollution as the normal hazards of everyday life, it didn't take long to guess that this was the greatest danger I had yet encountered in what seemed suddenly a very sheltered life. I had never braved the elements before in more than a walk on the moors with Ben in the rain—with the car

27

parked a few hundred yards away—or a snow-storm at Aynley House when the car got stuck and we had to walk to the village. There was nothing comparable in my life so far to my present danger. Mist and a madman. Whatever the character of the young man, this mountain was undoubtedly a killer. I remembered with dread all those regular accounts on television and in the newspapers of men losing their lives in the Cairngorms. If only Ben were here, wise, kind Ben, he would know what to do.

'Ben, oh Ben,' and I sat down and wept as I had done so often in the past, when he would come and reassure me, smiling, saying: 'There, there.'

But this time there was no Ben magically tuned in to my needs. Our wires had crossed and, blowing my nose, I realised Ben would at this moment be dining by candlelight with his new fiancée, watched over by Rona, who had doubtless overcome her feelings of guilt and betrayal during my absence to the tune of preparing a sumptuous meal for her future daughter-in-law. No, I wouldn't think about it and I told myself it was only tiredness and hunger that made me weep again. And the cold. It was getting colder by the second.

I wondered if it was too late in the year to be frozen to death. Then, opening my eyes, I saw a shadow which moved. For a fraction of time I thought a miracle had happened and somehow it would be Ben. . . .

The mist had thinned enough to reveal another benighted traveller. A girl, sitting on a rock, about six yards away. The rock must have marked the site of some ancient accident or tragedy, for there was a stone cross and a shrine like the ones I had encountered in parts of the Tyrol. Why had I presumed that the

Scots in these parts would be Presbyterian like my mother?

'Hello,' I called.

The girl turned with a questioning look. In that moment I was conscious only of her eyes. Extraordinary eyes, disproportionately large and glowing like bright candles in the pale delicate face, with its frame of fair hair escaping from the dark hooded cape which reached her feet.

'I'm lost. I was going to Deveron Castle.' I was thankful this didn't prompt her to ask what on earth, then, was I doing half-way up Cairn Dever? She merely nodded, pointed down the hill.

'There it is—look.' I could see the castle clearly. What a piece of luck. 'Just follow the sheep track. Don't be afraid, you'll be there safely in five minutes. I'll watch and see you get there. Hurry now, before the mist closes in again.' She held up a hand, cutting short my thanks. 'Hurry ...'

Once on the track, I stumbled, turned and saw her watching, a small hooded figure at the end of a tunnel of mist. As she seemed quite unperturbed by the appalling conditions, I concluded that she must be a shepherd's daughter and well used to coping with the mountain in all weathers.

It was difficult to explain, but I could still feel those astonishing eyes watching even when I reached the main road, but when I looked back there was nothing, both mist and girl had vanished. A thin watery sun touched with pearls of light the silver green of Cairn Dever, so that it looked benign, all soft curves and gentle ways, turning the roofless broken cottages clustered around me into romantic ruins. And suddenly Deveron Castle, its granite blushing softly in an after-glow of sunset.

Once again I was near, but not near enough. The castle stood at the end of a long weed-encrusted drive, ethereal and enchanting in the soft light, but between it and me were ornate gates. Tough strong gates and locked too. Enduring, as befitted gates locked for more than two hundred years.

As I stood tugging at them forlornly, I remembered Great-Uncle Fraser's story. Of Alexander Deveron who rode out at Prince Charlie's side in 1745 and, locking these gates behind him, gave instructions they were to remain so until he returned with his prince triumphant as king. But Alexander died at Culloden and the prince returned alone, defeated, with the Redcoats on his heels. The daughter of the house, the White Rose of Deveron, helped him escape, and paid for it with her life.

Romantic story it might be, I was too weary to feel anything but frustration and annoyance. There must be another way in and I found it fifty yards down the road. A more modern entrance once graced in Victorian times with a lodge, now a tumbled-down ruin, another ruin among many on this journey through fallen splendour. A twisting rhododendron drive gone wild in a profusion of colour, with a sylvan touch of wood alongside which, after a final twist and turn, emerged before a large unkempt lawn.

And there at last was my castle. First glance didn't suggest it had enjoyed much prosperity this century, but hadn't my aged relative warned me that it was too large for an old bachelor? True, the windows were shuttered, but hadn't he told me that he would need a note of warning to open the west wing and air it for my coming? I thought of that four-poster bed with gratitude. However, the setting sun suggested this was the west wing with its air of desolation, with slates

30

missing from roof and ominous cracks in its walls. Deveron Castle on closer inspection looked uneasily derelict.

I took a deep breath and squared my shoulders for a final assault. Having come this far, I mustn't be depressed by mere appearances. I mustn't let weariness and my imagination run riot again, cast me into gloomy foreboding. Soon I would be sitting down refusing a brace of partridge—it seemed like sacrilege, even hungry as I was, to eat such pretty birds. Worry over that moral issue seemed unnecessary when all the bird life evident at present was the rookery, busy and noisy above my head. Rooks stared down from roof and chimney of the castle too and congregated on every available ledge, their melancholy eyes sharp with malevolence. Maybe they had their reasons for suspicion of this newcomer in their midst; however, I suspected Great-Uncle Fraser was much too grand to set rook pie on the menu.

Following an overgrown path through a tumbled archway of once magnificent rambling roses, I emerged down some steps into the remains of a sunken arbour containing statues of gods and goddesses, all sadly green and pock-marked by the same lichen disease peculiar to ancient tombstones in country churchyards.

This charnel-house savour was so repellant I walked swiftly, eyes averted from a stage set with alarming aptitude for a horror movie. Turning another corner where all was neat and orderly, there by the castle was parked the complete anachronism. A large white and thoroughly modern caravan.

This must surely be the factor's office. I knocked on the door and, as I expected so late, there was no answer from within, but a dog's warning growl. Next,

I tried the side door of the castle and found it opened on to a spiral staircase.

'Hello,' I called. 'Uncle Fraser? Hello? Anyone at home?'

All was silent. Perhaps he was deaf. I clambered up a few rounds of spiral stairs into a large panelled gallery where corridors, yawning like bored open mouths, seemed to disappear in all directions.

'Hello!' But it was obvious that the place was deserted and had been so for some considerable time, by the evidence of last year's nests and bird lime on the panels and several broken windows.

It was growing darker and I didn't relish being lost in this eerie desolation any more than in the mist on Cairn Dever. Realising I had stumbled on the uninhabited part of the castle, I went out again and decided to reconnoitre. I soon gave up in despair and sat down beside my case, regarding the silent castle glowering above me, where even the rooks were now bedded. It was all faintly unnerving, this silence, as if I had suddenly found myself in a world deserted by all other living creatures.

I tried talking to Ben about it in my mind, but somehow tonight in this place I couldn't conjure him up, or make his unfailing benediction of 'There, there' seem real. Tonight there was always another face between him and me. A girl as yet unseen, with face and shape—according to Ben—like a Miss World candidate.

Deciding that my visit had unfortunately coincided with Great-Uncle's departure to foreign shores on Clan Deveron business, and that the servants probably slept in the village when he was not in residence, the sensible thing seemed to make my way there. It might also yield a fish-and-chip shop and an hotel where I would be welcomed gratis as the laird's great-niece. I headed down the lane to where car headlamps, gleaming like a migrating tribe of glow-worms, indicated a main road. But alas, in between was a blighted wilderness of heather, boulders and a barbed-wire fence that meant business.

Too discouraged to contemplate walking round two sides of a triangle again, I lay flat and wriggled through the wire. Dusting myself down, I set off determinedly across this no-man's-land towards Deveron village. Twenty yards further on my stumbling uneven progress was halted by an irate voice shouting:

'Come back. Come back at once. Do you hear me? This is private property . . .'

I looked back and saw a woman in the garden of a cottage which bordered the heath about fifty yards down the lane. She was waving wildly in my direction. 'Come back. Yes, you. Come over—this way. Don't you know it's dangerous? Do be careful . . .'

When I reached her garden, and clambered over the fence, I saw that under the headscarf she was elderly, but strong-looking, with white hair and a countrywoman's fresh healthy complexion. Despite reassuring smiles, she was certainly angry and unsuccessfully concealing something else remarkably like terror.

Apologising for being on private property, I said: 'I'm looking for Fraser Deveron.'

Her eyes travelled over my dishevelled appearance with interest and a flicker of amusement: 'Well, you certainly won't find him on the Murder Field.'

'The—what?'

'The Murder Field,' she said casually, and turning indicated that I follow her towards the house. 'He'll be home presently, I expect. He has to pass my front door on his way to the castle. You might as well come in and wait. I'll be making a cup of tea.'

She disappeared into the kitchen from which issued smells of baking that made me weak with hunger, after showing me into a pleasant sitting room where a fragrant fire of peat gleamed in the dusk. A grandfather clock briskly ticked away the minutes with the same cheery unconcern for the future that it must have shown for more than a hundred years, and I sat down facing pictures on the mantelpiece of the same young man in various stages, as baby, schoolboy and adult. It was an agreeable sensation to sit back and relax, safe from danger at last, out of the mist and knowing that I would be seeing Great-Uncle Fraser in a few moments—all those doubts and forebodings had been my usual overworked imagination.

'Come away then, here's some tea.' The woman set down shortbread, scones and raspberry jam. 'You help yourself now—I have baking in the oven to attend.'

I was on my second scone by the time she returned. She seemed pleased when I complimented her on the cooking and added : 'I haven't eaten since this morning. I'm afraid I got lost on Cairn Dever.'

'Just now?' she said, pouring another cup.

'Yes, I've just come down.'

She looked across at the window. 'Not in the mist, surely?'

'Oh yes, I met a girl who showed me the way.'

She stared at me, then replaced the teapot under its cosy. 'You're new to this place?'

'My mother was a Deveron, but she left long ago.'

'I see.' There was a moment's silence, then she said : 'You probably know all about the Murder Field, then, and how dangerous it is to disturb the spirits of the dead.'

'She didn't tell me.'

'Oh. Well, the heath hasn't been interfered with since the sixteenth century when there was a massacre of the Deverons by the Gordons. Those mounds you saw among the heather mark the common grave— even to this day, bones still come through to the surface.' She shook her head. 'Even before the Deveron massacre it was always an unlucky haunted place, in the old days it was a Pictish burial ground. There's a curse upon whoever disturbs the dead, especially a Deveron. And if he or she should hear the ghostly cries of the slain . . .'

At that moment a car shot past the window. 'Oh, that's Fraser Deveron now,' said the woman regretfully. 'I'd better not be keeping you.'

'Many thanks for the tea, I really appreciated it.'

'You're most welcome.' As I hesitated politely, she added. 'Go along, you'd better hurry and not let him escape you again.' She gave me a rather coy glance as we said goodbye.

As I approached the castle, a car came whizzing back down the lane. Behind the wheel I caught a glimpse of a pale face, under a familiar dark hood— and a puzzled expression as I waved to her in greeting. Surely the driver was the girl I had met at the shrine on Cairn Dever. She must be a tenant of Great-Uncle Fraser—that was why she knew the way down so well.

I knocked on the side door and waited. Somewhere inside a dog barked warningly. Light footsteps on the spiral stair were followed by a red setter who rushed out to greet me, every inch of him wagging with delight. Surely this was the dog I had seen earlier that

35

day, I thought, as I patted him and called him 'Good boy'.

'Actually he's a she and her name is Rusty,' said a cold voice above me, and turning, I looked into the flushed and angry countenance of the red-headed young man whose car I had borrowed. The resemblance to Robert the Bruce was more striking than ever. Only the axe was missing.

3

In the circumstances I took refuge in the only thing left to save my face. Pretending we had never met before, I regarded him stonily and said: 'Would you please tell Mr. Fraser Deveron that Miss Brent has arrived?'

He stared at me, hands on hips. 'And what might you be wanting *this* time? I'm Fraser Deveron,' he added grimly, and at that statement the coy manners of the lady at the cottage I had just left became abundantly clear.

'There must be some mistake.'

'Indeed there must, Miss Trouble. I might be a little confused, especially during the last two hours—thanks to you, but allow me to still know my own name. Who the devil are you, anyway?'

Something had certainly gone wrong. I had expected a man nearer seventy-two than twenty-two. I wondered what chicanery was afoot and, too late, my father's warning when long ago I expressed a romantic interest in the Deverons: 'They were a thoroughly bad lot, you're better off with honest hard-working Yorkshire kin. Only your mother was decent and respectable . . .' I did a nightmare addition of facts: the Murder Field, the terrified woman at the cottage and now this impostor calling himself Fraser Deveron.

'I'm looking for my great-uncle,' I said, conscious how lame it sounded.

'Are you now?' he said in tones of disbelief. 'You had better think of a better story for your presence on private property, to say nothing of stealing my car. That's a criminal offence, I'll have you know, especially as you abandoned it in a reckless fashion. The brake wasn't on properly and it ended up in the heather, with a broken spring, so I had to walk all the way back to the village. If the mist hadn't lifted I would have been up there all night.'

What a whopper. Obviously the girl I had just seen was an accomplice in some dark deed they were keen to keep quiet.

'Oh really,' I said casually. 'I met your friend, the girl driving the car, up Cairn Dever and she showed me the path to take down to the castle, as a matter of fact.'

He looked back over his shoulder to where the great mountain slumbered peacefully in the dying light. 'You met Morna—up there?'

'Of course. Soon after I—er, parked the car. She was waiting for someone—sitting on a rock, a sort of shrine. I asked her the way and at that moment the mist parted and I could see the path right down to the castle . . .'

'You must be mad,' he interrupted heavily. 'The girl you saw leaving here is Morna Keir, her father owns the Deveron garage and she was in charge of the

37

petrol pumps until he arrived back from Inverness half-an-hour ago. She could hardly be in two places at once, now could she?' After a moment's pause to let this extraordinary fact sink in, he continued : 'Besides, nobody, not even an experienced climber, would risk coming down the way you said *you* did, in weather like that. Another thing, Miss Trouble, I know every inch of Cairn Dever and there isn't any shrine on the mountain.' Head on side, he regarded me and asked quietly, 'What sort of game are you playing, coming here with a pack of lies? I think you had better clear off, before I change my mind and call the police. Pretending I'm your uncle . . .'

'I'm not pretending anything of the kind. My great-uncle came to visit us about five years ago. He'd be seventy or so now, long white hair, beard, moustache. A very distinguished old gentleman. Wearing the kilt. And he definitely owns this castle—at least,' and I had a moment's misgiving, 'he said he did.'

'Got it,' the young man snapped his fingers triumphantly. 'You must be the mysterious "Candid" the local bobby left a message from. Correct?' Digging into his pocket, he held up a piece of paper. 'This was under the caravan door.' I read it. Somewhat paraphrased it was the message I had arranged with the policeman at Muldoune Bridge. It had suffered some distortion in translation and brevity.

' "Arriving immediately. Candid." ' he read over my shoulder. 'Candid,' he snorted, 'what sort of a name is that? I thought it was a hoax, or somebody imagined I was in the secret service.'

'The name is Candida—Candida Brent.'

'My dear girl, you've been had. This place is thick with Deverons—all umpteenth cousins. Describe this old boy again.' When I did so, he thumped his fists together. 'Now I have it. You had a visit from Old Jamie—James Fraser Deveron—he was shepherd to the laird who lived in the castle here and they both had the same name.' He shook his head and chuckled. 'Well, well, old Jamie—a great romancer, a real character—fancy him being your great-uncle. Mind you, nobody but a Southron would believe a single word he said. Put him in the pub at night during the tourist season and they'd gather round him like bees at honey, while he lapped up free whiskies all round.'

The tale of free whiskies rang a familiar bell. 'I'd never met him before. He just walked in one day . . .'

At the end of my story, Fraser Deveron chuckled. 'Paris—and the Savoy, eh? My, my, what a tale. He really excelled himself that time.' Then he wasn't smiling any more and I detected a look of almost, well, compassion. He took my arm and said : 'Come along. We might as well have a seat in the caravan. I'm sorry the castle isn't quite ready to receive visitors.' Looking down into my face, he grinned rather disarmingly, I thought. 'It's all right, I promise not to eat you. I'll make you some coffee instead.' Ushering me in with Rusty bounding at my heels, he added with a gleam of devilment :

'Incidentally, what were you expecting to have done to you at the ski-hut? I was only there to deposit some things, I was merely being flippant about having to spend the night there.'

'You could have fooled me.'

He laughed. 'Mind you, it wouldn't be the first time I've been stranded up there.' And suddenly serious : 'Didn't you know there's a tradition of hospitality among Deverons which says that in the Glen no doors are ever locked, so that benighted travellers can always find shelter? There are few dishonest people in these parts. For hundreds of years property and life itself have been united in a grim game called the fight for survival. The castle is always open—we've only had one burglary in fifty years, and all they stole was a picture.' I thought of the way I had walked into the castle and remembered how carefully people locked their doors in Aynley, Yorkshire, and with very good reason for their caution.

'There's a law of chivalry, too,' he said gently. 'No man would take advantage of a girl who had to share a night with him out of necessity—unless, of course, she indicated that she was willing,' he added, with a mocking light in his eyes. 'And naturally, as we're indifferent about locking our house doors, we're rather careless about pocketing car keys.'

I had the grace to blush and murmur an apology. 'I hope I didn't do your car any lasting harm.'

'Let's say you didn't do it much good, but I've managed to get it down the hill and into the garage—it was due for other repairs—they can't all be laid at your door. Morna brought me home. How's about some coffee?'

The caravan was very comfortable, with much more living-space than the outside suggested. A sitting room with tiny dining annexe, a bedroom and even a shower. If I had thought of the interior of caravans at all, it was in terms of alfresco living, a kind of glorified camping. I didn't expect elegance, Wedgwood-blue plush carpeting and matching blue-and-white upholstery and curtains. A gas fire fitted snugly into its own redwood fireplace, whose veneers were repeated on cupboards and cabinets, interrupted by vast windows brooding over a panoramic landscape. From every angle the view was superb. There wasn't one television aerial in sight.

At the touch of a switch, soft music. At another, from a blank wall a stove descended, then as coffee bubbled, presto, another button and a table appeared, then the settee divided into two padded seats. Like some strange surrealist machine, each time a button was pressed, a transformation scene took place and everything turned upside down or inside out and changed into something else.

'How do you like my caravan?' asked its owner proudly.

'It's magnificent, but rather unnerving. I feel I had better keep my elbows close to my sides, in case it goes into reverse voluntarily, if I touch anything lethal. I had no idea caravans were like this.'

Fraser Deveron smiled. 'They aren't. I invented the gadgets in this one. I'm an architect and I've always been interested in providing compact flats for handicapped people and old folks living alone. I was asked to design some for a local council scheme and that's how my caravan evolved.' He stopped and gave me a look of compassion. 'Well, Miss Brent, sorry about your great-uncle. I'm afraid you've come too late. He's dead —went off to gather lambs during a snowstorm back in February. He never returned. We'll find him I expect, once the snow clears from the heights of Cairn Dever.'

'You mean—he's still up there—unburied?'

'I'm afraid so. The peak is covered in snow for all but three months of the year. They've searched the lower reaches, as far as they could, but there wasn't any trace of him. He could be right near the top.'

'How ghastly.'

He shrugged. 'It's a situation not unknown here in the glen. Besides, don't feel badly about it, because, give old Jamie his due, it was the way he would have wanted to go. He loved the mountains and the heather, he had always a terror of getting old and help-less and dying in his bed. "Give me the earth around me, the stars over my head," he'd say. And he knew the mettle of his enemy, for he battled with it every day of his life. The mountains here are killers.' He wag-ged an admonishing finger at me. 'Make no mistake about it, young lady.' Rusty put her head on his knee and made imploring sounds.

'All right, old girl, you'll get your walk soon.' He grinned at me. 'We're creatures of habit, Rusty and me. We usually take a walk down to the pub and this clever girl knows the time.'

I took the hint and stood up. 'Thanks for the coffee and for being so helpful. I'd better be on my way.'

'Where's that?'

'Back to Yorkshire.'

'Yorkshire—that's a long journey. Where have you come from?'

'Inverness.'

He looked puzzled. 'Deveron's well out of your route. Shouldn't you have gone into Aberdeen and taken the train from there?'

'I should—but I missed my bus at Muldoune Bridge earlier today.'

'Really? I wish I'd known. I was meeting a pros-pective client who is considering a sixteenth-century castle, if I can restore it for him.'

I smiled. 'As a matter of fact, I saw you walking along the street with Rusty.'

'How on earth did you remember me?'

'Let's say you both have very distinctive colouring.'

He ran a hand through his hair. 'Red, carrot, ginger—I've been called them all.' He sighed. 'It's a Deveron family failing. You were lucky to evolve into chestnut. There are Red Deverons and Black Deverons, nothing in-between. I always prayed each night when I was a wee boy that it would darken with age, but if anything it only got brighter. If I'd been a girl,' he added fiercely, 'I would have dyed it, a nice mouse-brown, fine and inconspicuous.'

'You shouldn't worry—it's very distinguished. When I first saw you I thought how beautifully you both blended with the setting of hills and glens. I thought you looked like Robert the Bruce as I imagined him, red hair and all.'

He smiled shyly. 'That's the nicest, most flattering remark I've had about my hair—and from an English lady too.' He made it sound as if flattery and living south of the border were somehow incompatible. 'So tell me what happened after you missed your bus.'

Pride stopped me saying that I hadn't enough money to continue my journey. 'I was told there wouldn't be another bus until morning. The police took pity on me, inveigled a lift from a pop group to Deveron and I decided to renew old acquaintance with—Jamie, as you call him.'

'You're not much better off? There's no bus from here until morning, either, so perhaps you could stay the night with Jeannie Deveron—you must have passed her cottage down the lane. She does bed and breakfast during the season—I'm sure she'll be able to take you.' When I explained that I had met her, but that I really couldn't afford to stay, he said: 'Don't worry, you'll be Deveron's guest. Come along, we'll walk you down. Right, Rusty.'

Jeannie beamed on Fraser and I suspected from the coy looks in my direction she suspected that I was his girl friend, for she was only too delighted to offer me a bed at his request.

'No trouble at all, Mr. Fraser. I always have a bedroom ready and aired. I'll be pleased to put Miss—Brent up. Come away in, my dear.'

As Fraser lingered at the gate, I made another half-hearted apology. 'Sorry I caused you so much trouble —with the car and everything.'

'I dare say we'll both survive.' Smiling he bowed—rather gallantly, I thought—over my hand. 'I'll bid you good night and a safe journey home to Yorkshire.'

Later I enjoyed a simple but delicious meal of bacon-and-egg at a table set with delicate china and a white lace-edged tablecloth. Considering the prevalence of embroidery about the room, I guessed it had all come from the same hand and, feeling the warmest I had been in days, I complimented Mrs. Deveron on her needlework and her cooking.

She seemed pleased and as I accepted a third cup of tea, remarked: 'So you're moving on tomorrow? Well now, it's fine that you managed to see Mr. Fraser after all.' She waited politely, then added: 'He doesn't get many visitors, you know, keeps very much to himself.' With a heavy sigh she continued: 'Aye, I recall the old days my father talked about, when every family in the glen had at least two people serving at the castle. And in the season extra maids and waiters came by the score from miles around. Especially when the old king—Edward the Seventh—Bertie, they all called him, arrived with his retinue. Young Mr. Fraser's grandmother was a great favourite with him, some said there was good reason, for if truth were to be told she wasn't an earl's daughter at all, but one of his illegitimate children.'

Pausing to let me digest this delicious piece of scandal, Mrs. Deveron shook her head sadly: 'Great days they were, right enough. With not an empty bed to be found in the glen, and all those ruined cottages at the foot of Cairn Dever with roofs to them and peat fires glowing—aye, smoke from every chimney there was. Such grand vegetable gardens too. Now there's nothing but desolation and a stricken glen with its poor castle crumbling away. And our young master working like the poorest farmhand, every spare day's holiday he gets, trying to straighten out the awful mess his grandfather and his father left him.' She looked across at me : 'But I expect you're familiar with the story.'

As I nodded vaguely, I remembered with shame my patronising attitude, my unforgivable behaviour to the laird of Deveron. If I had been a little less thick, I should have realised that the police at Muldoune Bridge might reasonably be expected to have a more accurate picture of the Deverons than I did. Their remark about the laird—Fraser Deveron—dying ten years ago, and leaving a 'laddie' to inherit, should have aroused my suspicions. And I could have saved myself an unnecessary journey, a terrifying experience on a mist shrouded mountain, to say nothing of considerable embarrassment all round and breaking the spring of Fraser Deveron's car.

Miss Trouble, he'd called me. Suddenly I was determined I mustn't ever meet him again. If I caught that morning bus, there was little chance of any further red faces.

'. . . crippled with arthritis, crippled in spirit too, he was, after she went away. Aye, there's some say the old laird died of a broken heart, poor gentleman.'

In my confused state of mind I realised I had missed some vital part of Jeannie Deveron's story. I was sitting close to a handsome and very modern recording unit, idly looking at pop discs which denoted Jeannie Deveron had a somewhat incongruous taste in music.

'That belongs to my son,' she said sharply, as if to

45

command my wandering attention. Then she continued with a sigh : 'And so it goes on. Now young Mr. Fraser is dedicated to paying off the family debts, restoring Deveron and the castle to their former prosperity. He's determined to make his life here as his ancestors did. Meanwhile, all we see of him are short stays in the caravan whenever he can get away from his Glasgow job, doing small repairs to the castle, busy all the time.'

She paused and looked at me very pointedly. 'As I said, he doesn't get many visitors.' She was so plainly curious, I said : 'It wasn't Mr. Fraser I came to visit. It was my great-uncle, old Jamie Deveron, the laird's shepherd. I gather he's been missing on Cairn Dever since February.'

After a silence when even the grandfather clock seemed to hold its breath she said : 'That is what we believe.' Another silence, then she added : 'Is that why you came to Deveron, because of the old man's disappearance?' And without waiting for an answer : 'I never knew he had any family, especially away down in England. Who sent you? Nobody has enquired about him until now.'

'Nobody sent me. He's all the kin I have and when I missed my bus at Muldoune Bridge I thought I'd take the opportunity and visit him. I haven't seen him for five years.' I wondered as I spoke why I felt both apologetic and rather defensive.

'He didn't leave anything, you know,' she said sharply. She pointed to the grandfather clock. 'There's only that and he gave it to me to settle some debts. I have the receipt somewhere.'

She was about to jump up and look for it when I said : 'Please don't bother. I believe you.'

'He had no money, nothing,' she said belligerently,

and sensing hostility and probably a large number of unpaid debts which had stung her into this sudden unfriendliness, I decided it would be opportune to change the subject.

Indicating the photographs on the mantelpiece, I asked pleasantly: 'Is this your son?'

Jeannie clenched her fists. 'Yes, it is.' She looked at me narrow-eyed and demanded: 'What do you know about Joe? Did he send you here? Where is he?' When I replied that I had no idea, she mumbled an apology, but it was too late to conceal that she was distraught and that my questions about her son had stirred another version of the wild creature who had raged at me earlier for being on the Murder Field. I was sorry for her, but suddenly I was tired too. I didn't want any more third degree, just to retire to a quiet room and sleep.

Standing up with all the dignity I could muster, I said firmly: 'I'm very tired. You must excuse me.'

'All right,' she said grudgingly. 'Come and I'll show you your room.'

I followed her upstairs to a Victorian bedroom, neat and clinically white from bedspread to curtains which she carefully drew closed.

'Please don't open them. The sun fades everything. Then there are moths.' She paused hopefully. 'You would be afraid of moths flying in?'

I yawned. 'Not really.'

She seemed disappointed. 'Well, some say they are the spirits of the murdered from the field across there.' She paused with her hand on the door. 'Incidentally, to see—or hear—the murder means death, if you're a Deveron.'

I was almost too tired to think, certainly too tired to imagine battles fought so long ago. However, some time during that night I dreamed—and vividly—for when I awoke it was to hear the sounds of guns, the screams of men and horses.

Bewilderment and fear gave place to anger as I sat up in bed and switched on the light. The sounds continued and I decided that Mrs. Deveron must be listening to the radio, since there was no television. I tried to sleep again, but the off-stage din remained unabated. Perhaps Mrs. Deveron was a little deaf, for the sound was unnervingly close and I wondered how I could tactfully ask her to turn it down.

After a while of hoping that the programme would come to an end, or at least give way to some soothing music, I stretched over to look at my watch.

It said four o'clock. She couldn't be listening to a radio play at four a.m. I sprang out of bed, pulled back the curtains. The glow of light announced the dawn of another day. Down below me was Murder Field, where the dead lay heaped in common graves and their bones still crept through to the surface, as if the owners uneasily stirred.

I shivered. It was a scene of profound desolation, with early morning mist moving slowly, transforming heather hillocks into the watchful shapes of crouching men among the boulders. Then I realised, it was no radio I heard, but Murder Field, with its ghostly battle still raging, heard but quite unseen.

4

I awoke with sunshine flooding the room, through the curtains I had hastily redrawn after my alarming glimpse of the Murder Field at dawn. On a chair by the window lay my present for Ben. Somehow it reproached me as I realised for the first time since our break-up I hadn't given him a thought for twelve hours. Usually my awakening thought was that losing him had been a bad dream, followed swiftly by the aching realisation that it wasn't a dream at all. He had gone. . . .

Mrs. Deveron tapped on the door. 'I brought you a cup of tea.' Her friendly smile drained away as setting down the breakfast tray she noticed the disarranged curtains. Swiftly she drew them close, shutting out the sunlight. 'I thought I told you, Miss Brent—it's dangerous to open the curtains. *They* were very busy out there last night, didn't you hear them?'

'Who were busy?' I asked sleepily.

'The Deverons, of course.' She sounded disappointed. '*They* never rest, the dead don't need sleep,' she added sharply, and marched out banging the door behind her, and leaving me to mull over this surprising statement with my tea and biscuits. Later I went downstairs with an hour to spare before the bus passed the lodge gates.

Suddenly the whole idea of a ghostly battle at Murder Field was utterly ridiculous, too absurd to mention. Sunlight streaming through the windows, the normality of a breakfast table set most attractively before a glowing peat fire, suggested a more logical reason than the supernatural for the sounds of battle that had disturbed me. I wondered if the plumbing were at fault and half-asleep I could have imagined those blood-curdling sounds.

'You are definitely leaving today?' asked Mrs. Deveron. 'You haven't changed your mind?' When I told her I was going she nodded : 'Just as well, because I need the room. I have another guest arriving unexpectedly.' She looked down at me with folded arms. 'That will be two pounds, if you please. And I prefer cash.'

My hand flew to my empty purse as embarrassed I realised Fraser must have forgotten to mention that I was Deveron's guest. Taking a deep breath I said : 'I'm very sorry, Mrs. Deveron, but I can't pay you at all at the moment. I left my wallet in the woollen mill at Muldoune Bridge and I understand from the local police that the owners are away for the weekend.' Then with the greatest dignity I could muster I handed over Ben's sweater in its now crumpled box. 'Perhaps you will accept this as security. When I get back I'll send you the money, then perhaps you'd be kind enough to post this parcel for me. Here's my address . . .'

She took the parcel and regarded it with some doubt, giving it a shake, as if there might be some trick and she would open it to find it empty.

'Allow me.' Taking it back, I tore off string, wrappings, and held up the sweater. 'This should more than meet my debt to you. Here's the receipt—so you can always take it back if I don't pay. The shop said they would refund the money if it didn't fit.'

Examining it she seemed impressed and said that her terms were usually cash, but she *supposed* it would be all right this once. Without my asking, she produced the bus fare into Aberdeen and added that I could return that too with the postage.

She went into the kitchen to refill the teapot, leaving me staring out of the window at a landscape of such charm, I regretted not knowing Fraser Deveron was its laird. At least I could have begged a conducted tour of his castle and the glen, for the parts of both so briefly glimpsed suggested they might be worth closer inspection.

There were voices in the kitchen and footsteps.

'Anyone at home?' And there he was with Rusty at his heels. Accepting Mrs. Deveron's offer of a cup of tea, he sat down opposite me and talked as I finished breakfast. Before his genial friendliness, embarrassment at our earlier unfortunate encounter vanished and my resolution to stay out of his way seemed absurd. Surprised to see him, I also found I was genuinely delighted too.

How ridiculous that I had ever considered his motives sinister, for in the morning light he looked young and attractive, with his red hair boyishly untidy, eyes sparkling as he joked with my landlady. Could it be that he had pleasing manners with women, hitherto unsuspected—judging by the shine he brought to her normally solemn countenance?

As I watched them, there was something else too, something vulnerable about him. His rather worn shoes gallantly polished, the jacket with its patched elbows, I found terribly touching in the light of what Jeannie had told me. I wondered how much he earned as an architect and it seemed unfair that so young a man should have to mortgage his life repairing a ruined castle and restoring a forgotten glen—in an attempt to pay off debts not of his own making.

I looked away hastily as he turned in my direction, afraid he would read my thoughts too clearly.

'When are you leaving?' he asked.

51

'In about ten minutes.'

He put down his cup. 'Right. I'll walk you down to the bus-stop.' As we walked down the lane, as if explanation were needed, he said: 'I thought I would look in to say goodbye . . . Hey, wait a minute. Aren't you a piece of luggage short—or have you been diligently repacking?'

I told him about the lost wallet, what an idiot I had been leaving it in the shop and how that was my reason for coming to Deveron.

'I thought we had agreed you were to be my guest?' He paused and added: 'Anyway, what happens when you get to the station and you haven't a ticket for the journey to York?'

'I'm hoping that British Railways will lend a sympathetic ear to my story. A word with my boss at Perseus Plastics should do the trick.' I didn't add that a word with Ben would move mountains.

'What a trusting soul you are,' said Fraser. 'Hold on,' and he dashed back to the cottage. A moment later he returned, thrusting the box into my hand. 'There now—I've paid Jeannie for you. Yes, I insist. And take this.' He thrust five pounds into my hand. 'Go on—it'll save embarrassment if they don't believe your story; besides, you might want to eat on the journey. Take it,' he said firmly. 'You can send it back later.'

I was still protesting and he was still adamant when we reached the bus-stop where I decided on gracious acceptance.

Indicating the box, which I now clutched fondly, he said: 'For the man in your life, I expect?' When I said yes, he looked rather pointedly at my left hand. 'I wondered if you were engaged. That's a most unusual ring. Sixteenth-century Florentine, isn't it?'

52

'Yes, we bought it in an antique shop in Rome. I never wanted a conventional three-diamond affair and this one is so pretty. It was love at first sight—a perfect fit too. Ben said it had been waiting for us.'

'He's a very lucky fellow,' said Fraser with conventional politeness.

A brisk denial of the engagement would have been so easy, but suddenly I wanted to bask in the pretence that Ben was mine—for just a little longer. After all, Fraser need never know. . . .

He was chatting knowledgeably about the ring which Ben had indignantly refused to have returned to him, despite its value, for the huge ruby was real and I decided that alteration to fit some other finger was an urgent necessity. His new fiancée would doubtless eye it as showing both lack of taste and a considerable failure of pride.

'Apart from a natural desire to get back to the man in your life, are you in a terrible hurry to leave?' asked Fraser, concentrating on kicking a stone in his path with boyish enthusiasm—or perhaps to cover an attack of shyness. 'People around here are honest, as I told you yesterday. Only one burglary in fifty years and all they took was a painting. I'm sure you'll get your wallet back as soon as the owners of the mill return.' He paused and smiled, rather wistfully I thought. 'It isn't often one meets even distant relations. Or they are quite ghastly when one does. I expect we're umpteenth cousins. Look, why don't you stay over for a couple of days—or will he be missing you too much?'

I thought of how I dreaded returning to Aynley House, to Perseus Plastics, to meeting Debbie and wearing a false cheerful smile, pretending I was very broad-minded and still had my place in the Armstrong family whatever happened between Ben and me. Pretending to be happy when my heart ached with misery seeing them together, weighed down by the falsity of the role I had chosen to play—an air of nonchalence that I couldn't afford to relinquish for a moment. It wasn't as if Rona would be worried, or even expecting me back until tomorrow. The cottage I had looked over for her had been unsuitable. I had only decided to rush back because I felt so lost and alone, even worse away from Ben and Rona than I felt with them just now—if such feelings were possible, or such misery imaginable.

A yellow bus trundled slowly round the corner—I stepped back.

'I'd love to stay. Thank you very much.' The bus hurtled past and my decision was made.

'Good,' said Fraser. 'And the weather's improved too—Deveron's smiling on you. Well, now that you've come, you might as well see something of the land of your ancestors.'

'I'd better phone York.'

There was a telephone box in the village and while Fraser waited outside, my heart pounded anxiously as I dialled the Aynley number. What if Ben answered? I longed to hear his voice and at the same time dreaded his polite enquiries, a far-off charm that would turn him into a stranger. I was about to replace the receiver when Mrs. Moody, the housekeeper, answered.

'No, no, Miss Candida. They're all away for the day, with the American lady. Yes, indeed I'll tell them you called. That's grand you meeting some Deveron cousins. Makes a nice change, doesn't it?'

'What's the weather like?'

'Pouring down cats and dogs, it is,' she said cheerfully. 'Never stopped raining since the American lady arrived.' And I wondered how long would pass before she would be 'Mrs. Debbie' or 'Mrs. Armstrong' and how much the old housekeeper guessed about the real situation.

However, I'm afraid that, replacing the receiver, I was human enough to feel that whatever winds blew in Aynley House I was delighted that the sun shone in Deveron. And as we walked back down the road, in the warmth of a calm spring morning, I said with a sigh :

'How lovely it is. Listen to the birds all agleam and the hills singing.'

'Surely it's the other way round?' said Fraser, laughing. As our hands met briefly, I was dazzled by the first feelings of pure happiness I had known since Ben stopped loving me—and even the dog bounding ahead, excitedly exploring the hedgerows, had a part in that sudden leap of joy. I remember looking fondly at Fraser, even hopefully. Besotted as I was with Ben's image, he didn't attract me in the least. All I longed for was an oasis of friendship, warm but platonic, un-emotional and undemanding.

It was wonderful to be young and carefree as I had not been in years, a mood I had almost forgotten, ready to dance and sing in one of those rare shafts of delight which for no reason at all appear like rain-bows after the worst of human storms, and make the possibility of tomorrow's personal disasters remote and of not the slightest importance.

'Might as well deposit your case back with Jeannie,' said Fraser.

'Oh—I'd forgotten, I can't stay there tonight, she told me she needs the room.'

'That's awkward. We have a pub in the village, but it's non-residential. Deveron isn't geared up for tourists these days, especially as it's off the main road. Let's not worry, I'm sure I can persuade Jeannie to find you a corner somewhere.' I had a sudden revulsion at cashing in on Mrs. Deveron's fondness for the laird of Deveron, even to the extent of taking in an unwelcome and inconvenient extra guest.

'I'd rather not . . .'

'Oh, don't be silly. Weren't you comfortable there last night?'

'She told me an extraordinary story about this place' —we were approaching the Murder Field—'and I'm afraid it gave me nightmares.'

Fraser laughed. 'Oh, the old massacre. You mustn't take any notice of Jeannie. She's a bit of a witch, but a good sort really, despite her relish for ghoul and gore. She tells some very good yarns. I'm afraid when people have been born and bred to the glen for generations—and never left it for long—the past walks hand-in-hand with the present, even when yesterday can be reckoned in two or three centuries.'

'Have you ever seen anything?'

Fraser shook his head. 'Alas, no, but not from lack of trying. It's not that I don't believe, I try to keep an open mind, but I think I'm completely insensitive to psychic phenomena. I must admit when I was a boy I spent hours on Murder Field, willing something to happen. With all those ghosts of my murdered ancestors roaming outside the castle, to say nothing of the White Rose on the prowl inside, I felt at a distinct disadvantage never being able to brag of having seen or heard anything more remarkable than a mouse scuttling behind the panelling. Perhaps it was as well, because for a Deveron to see the White Rose means death. Hardly an incentive to be psychic, is it? I hadn't so many relatives that I could afford to be careless about them. Most of the time I only had my father.'

He had his hand on the cottage gate and I said: 'Look, I don't want to bother Mrs. Deveron. Perhaps there's someone else in the village who would give me bed and breakfast.'

'All right.' His accompanying look made me wonder how much of my terror and reluctance he understood. 'I'm sure Morna will be able to help.'

I had almost forgotten Morna's mysterious behaviour. Why hadn't she admitted to Fraser that she rescued me from the mist of Cairn Dever? And like an icy cloud across the sun of my day it brought the first feeling of unease—that there was something going on in this glen that I didn't understand, something dangerous. I was prepared to dismiss Murder Field and its noisy ghosts as a nightmare brought about by the fanciful tales of Jeannie Deveron, who might well be harmlessly mad, but there was something about Fraser's friend, Morna Keir, and her presence on the mountain that I found inexplicably disturbing.

Her sudden appearance and how cold I had been. I remembered the strange luminosity of her eyes had frightened me and even as I walked away from her I had been acutely aware of them watching me. Perhaps my preoccupation had been the reason I couldn't recall *in detail* my flight down the mountain. In retrospect the whole encounter was tinged with a curious sense of unreality. Yet, seeing her a second time, she was just a pretty girl and I wondered uneasily if the mist had been responsible for her first pale and unearthly appearance.

When we reached the caravan I apologised for my earlier behaviour. 'It was very sweet of you to be so kind, because I did behave badly—honestly, I never

57

thought I'd be able to look you in the eye again. I had no idea that you were the laird of Deveron until the lady at the cottage told me.'

Fraser smiled. 'I don't blame you for not knowing. Personally, I never think of myself in so elevated a role. I'm really just a glorified farmer with rather more wilting non-productive property than I can manage. I think I'm better at building multi-storey flats than taking on this sort of job sometimes.'

'When Mrs. Deveron told me what you were doing for the glen I thought it was marvellous. I envy someone with such dedication.'

He shook his head. 'You make it all sound much grander, much more noble, than I think of it—as just a job of work to be done, a duty to the people who suffered with my family in their misfortunes. When the Deverons came down they brought with them an entire community, unsuited to any other life than that of their ancestors. Beside the misfortunes of the Deveron family—which were all of their own making —the real tragedy seemed to me those small families being uprooted. Children who emigrated never to return and sank without trace in great cities—where they imagined finding pavements made of gold. I realised that besides national disasters such personal tragedies are commonplace, but in some way each one registered on my conscience, because I was intimately related to the Deverons who had caused it all.'

He stopped and smiled. 'Sorry to deliver you a long lecture—I get carried away on my pet theme. Come along and see the castle.'

He opened the door and we climbed the spiral staircase to the gallery. Its ruin was even more pathetic with the gleam of sunshine coming through the long windows. There was no softening evening light to hide a tale of poverty, desolation and imminent disaster. The tale was repeated room after room, some with furnishing still, with chairs and faded upholstery, curtains once brocade and beautiful now tattered and ancient, made the story all more heart-breaking. This parody of magnificence, where ghosts of past days lingered still in the remains of grandeur, a handsome ceiling, a chandelier, a canopied bed . . .

Fraser pointed to it and said : 'Built into the castle in 1548 and as it could never be negotiated down the spiral staircase there it will remain until the walls fall down.'

Several other rooms told a similar story, retaining the original sixteenth-century furniture because it had been built inside the castle and was too unwieldy for removal as the tastes and fashions of the centuries had changed.

'Not that way,' said Fraser, as I began to walk in the direction of where I imagined the long gallery lay. 'You can get fearfully disorientated with all these corridors. Actually there is a pattern to them. When in doubt keep an eye on Rusty there—she knows the way, clever girl. The original Alexander Deveron who designed the castle, the first architect in the family— and the last—until I came along, must have had a rare sense of humour. I have a great fondness for old Alexander, I always think we would have had a lot in common, for he was as much an inventor in his way as I am. Only I design space-saving gadgets and mechanical devices for handicapped people while he designed life-saving gimmicks. The castle was originally a fortified house and if you take a wrong turning in these narrow corridors, which are in a maze pattern, you can wander about for hours, always returning to the same spot.'

'Do you spend much time in Deveron?'

'Every available holiday, long weekends and so forth. Alas, it doesn't seem to make a great deal of difference, not even a small bite into the amount of work to be accomplished single-handed.' He sighed. 'I have one week left, then it's back to Glasgow and my modern flats. If only I could take six months, a year off, it would make so much difference. I'm afraid most of the things that need doing scarcely get further than the drawing-board stage and I doubt whether I'll ever be able to afford to pack up architecture and a steady income. Maintaining the place once I do get it into shape will need considerably more money than the kind I can lay my hands on.'

When I asked him what sort of plan he worked on he said : 'Well, I aim to make the roof and the outer walls sound first of all, then one floor at a time. Eventually it will all be habitable again. Of course, the finished version will be so enormous I couldn't possibly occupy more than a few rooms. But I could let it in flats and the rent would help pay for the restoration of the next rooms, the next floor and so on. At the moment I'm concentrating on the oldest part, the master bedroom and the gallery and the solar room. Perhaps enough to live in myself and sell the caravan...'

As he talked I watched him with compassion, realising that he would be only a little younger than Ben. Ben could have restored this castle, for there was nothing ever defeated him. But Ben had been born old and wise and just a shade ruthless. I suspected that Fraser was far from ruthless and quite candidly I couldn't see him ever achieving his dream.

He was talking of money in terms that neither Rona nor Ben ever gave a second thought to spending on one antique or a painting. Rona refurnished Aynley House, one room each year, at a cost of sometimes several thousand pounds, firmly disposing of furniture and carpets still elegant merely because she was tired of them or they were no longer in the latest fashion. Both bought new cars every second year and flew to the States sometimes four times annually and oftener than that to the villa in Majorca, the flat in Rome. Their poverty was being in need of ten thousand pounds, while to others it was being in need of ten.

Suddenly with crystal clarity I saw my share of life in their pseudo-Tudor mansion, where money was spent feverishly, as if it too was going out of style. True, consciences were readily salved with lavish gifts to Oxfam, United Nations and the Wild Life Fund, but now it seemed an existence rather shameful and worthless by comparison to this young man's spartan efforts to right an old wrong not of his own making.

5

Our tour was interrupted by the sound of a car horn far below. Fraser poked his head out of one of the windows and a man in dungarees shouted: 'Mr. Keir said I was to bring you this car, sir, but he'll need it later. We're being as quick as we can with yours, but there's a part to come from Inverness.'

As I followed Fraser downstairs and out into the

sunlight, he turned smiling and said: 'You're very silent. Come now, don't look so apologetic. It isn't all your fault that the car's disabled—honestly, it was in poor shape before we met.'

'If you'd let me pay my share of the damage then . . .'

'Nonsense—wouldn't think of it.'

The red Volkswagen was a distinct improvement in age and comfort to the noisy Land-Rover. Soon we were driving away up through twisting pine-clad lanes to where even the forests ended far below us and only the wild moors remained. Twice Fraser stopped so that I could look down on the lovely panorama of Strathdon spread out before us in hill, field and croft, while Bennachie brooded magnificently over all and, at his shoulder, only slightly smaller but far more sinister, snow-capped Cairn Dever. And behind them both towered the silver ranges of the Cairngorm Mountains.

'It's rather early,' said Fraser. 'Care to walk?'

From the back seat, Rusty pricked up her ears at this invitation and with an elegant yawn swept out and, nose down, busily occupied herself on the trail of invisible rabbits. We followed her along the dried-up bed of a stream until it emerged in a great natural amphitheatre nestling among high hills where only a fretful wind sighed in the heather. Remote from human contact, man's hand had built no walls, had touched no blade of grass, nor carved his name on rock or tree to mark his passing. Here was a world newly-minted, as it had been on that first morning when God created it, with a stream gurgling, idle and unseen, and heathery ridges broken by occasional peat hags.

After a lifetime spent in the crowded noisy world of a Yorkshire factory district and the last few years in the science-fiction surroundings of Perseus

Plastics, such silence, such emptiness, overpowered the senses by their intensity. Even Aynley House, my home, supposedly in a remote village, was yet never far from the distant thunder of the M1, the smoke of factory chimneys dotted the horizons, and the scream of jets left vapour trails overhead. But this was different. Here was a setting where the world waited to begin, where the players still mingled silently in the wings awaiting their cues to take the stage.

I shivered, wondering whether Man might not, after all, be called upon to play the main part in the drama. Perhaps such a role was destined for some stranger race that preceded him, with origins unrecorded in history.

Suddenly the empty sky had a single occupant and the curtain had arisen, the story had begun. High above the black heather-clad ridge, its sharp-angled skyline blurred as a Turner landscape dazzled in unexpected sunshine, a bird flew. Magnificently it took the centre of the stage, hovering a moment to let its golden head catch the sunlight. Then, sure of an audience again, it glided, wings set, across and away from us, such grace and splendour leaving no hint of deadly purpose. The reason for its search, when it swooped and presumably found its prey—red deer calves dappled among heather.

Fraser grasped my arm. 'Listen. Danger's over . . .' And the silence had gone. The world that had held its breath while death hovered majestically, now erupted in the sound of peewits with a nest close at hand, whose occupants urgently demanded food. Harrassed parents took to the wing only feet away from us and the heather became alive with the small suppressed hummings, murmurings and scratchings of its unseen life. Somewhere a dog barked . . .

At Fraser's heels, all frivolity now set aside, Rusty lay silent, patiently awaiting his first command. Motionless, her eagerness betrayed by a mere flick of tail.

Fraser, following my glance, shook his head and said : 'A dog-fox—a warning bark, I think. Our eagle has reached his territory. Hear that?' There was another shriller bark. 'That's almost certainly the vixen warning her cubs. I hope she was in time—there's always plenty of carrion about for our eagle and her young not to go hungry.' He sighed. 'It's too lovely a day to be marred by the smallest tragedy. One wants everything to live and be happy.'

'Yes, I agree. It reminds me of a poem :

"Lord, I do fear
Thou'st made the world too beautiful this year.
My soul is all but out of me . . ." '

I paused, uncertain, embarrassed, and Fraser, with a hand on my arm, continued gently :

' "Let fall
No burning leaf; prithee, let no bird call." '

'How strange that you should know that one. So few people of our generation appreciate Edna St. Vincent Millay. My father met her once in New York and she gave him a signed copy of her poems. I discovered her quite by accident one rainy day a few years ago.'

'So did I.' And I had a sudden vision of us both in our separate worlds, on a day with the wind and the rain making play outside impossible, mooching through bookshelves and then lying on a rug in front of the fire, reading a book of poems perhaps the same edition, oblivious of all else but the magic and music of words.

The idea was alarmingly vivid and I looked at Fraser and thought: A poet shared, this is the first bond between us. Then I realised it wasn't the first, we shared an instinctive love of beauty, of the country-side. I wished Ben could have been like this. Ben who preferred to go sophisticated places where he could see, and be seen. Publicity was good for business, one must be made aware, he said.

As is often the case with people who see each other unexpectedly revealed, the sudden intimacy threw a blight over our conversation as we went back to where the car waited, a fat red beetle crouching against the brooding greyness of an approaching storm.

Over lunch in the Deveron Hotel, Fraser talked about my great uncle and the picture that emerged would have surprised Rona, who had succumbed to the image he presented to us on his visit: An elderly eccentric but distinguished Scottish laird, just the kindly old man to stay with for the shooting some year. Old Jamie, Deveron's shepherd, shorn of his illusions of grandeur, was the local drunk, never to be seen without his bottle of whisky.

'I can only suppose he came by an illicit store when he was night-watchman at the distillery,' said Fraser. 'He used to live in Jeanie's cottage, but when he went away to this job for a couple of years it was unoccupied, the garden all overgrown. Once it had belonged to Jeannie's father—she had been born there, and her son Joe. As she had been widowed a few years back, I negotiated with the absent tenant to let her occupy it. Old Jamie agreed, in principle, as he had a bothy up the glen. However, once he had the drink in him, he would come back down into Deveron and try to forcibly evict Jeannie and Joe, who was a pretty tough character.'

I remembered the pictures I had seen of him, and asked where he was now. 'He took himself off to Canada a few months back, promising to find a place for his mother and himself.' Fraser shook his head. 'I've no great faith in that young man, however, he was always a wide boy, one of these lads who sail pretty close to the wind but never actually get caught at anything dishonest. Of course, Jeannie thinks the world of him and she begged me to give him a job during the holidays, helping inside the castle. That was all very well until I found that not only the wind was accounting for the falling slates and that Master Joe was doing a nice line in selling my slates to a scrap dealer. I didn't want to make a fuss and distress Jeannie, so I asked him politely to depart and found him a pilfer-proof job. However, this didn't last long before he decided to emigrate. I find with the castle that I work best alone—perhaps I have an instinct for what is wrong, an inbuilt radar . . .'

The conversation switched back to the castle and Fraser described his trials and tribulations restoring the master bedroom.

'Is that the one with the four-poster?' When he said yes, I continued : 'How gorgeous—do you know it's always been my ambition to sleep in a bed with curtains. It was something Great-Uncle promised me when I came to Deveron. He said Mary, Queen of Scots had slept there.'

Fraser chuckled. 'Rubbish. Every four-poster in Scotland has a legend of Mary sleeping there. Down in England it's always Queen Elizabeth. Nobody seems happy with an ancient bed unless it has royal associations.'

'Well, with or without a queen having rested there, I'd still adore to sleep in one.'

'Would you really?' He sounded surprised. 'Maybe I can arrange that some time—to make up for not being your great-uncle.' He looked at his watch. 'Will you excuse me, I have to phone Morna.'

While he was away I thought about Morna, wondering whether they were in love and would get married once Fraser could afford the luxury of a wife, after he had achieved his major ambition of heading castle and glen in the general direction of rebirth and prosperity. From the evidence of my eyes, it seemed a forlorn hope.

As if he guessed my thoughts, when he returned he talked about Morna and her family, the only incomers to Deveron for many years. He spoke of her in obvious tones of admiration and affection and added: 'Of course, Morna's great-grandmother was a Deveron— the glen has completely captivated her, she's full of enthusiasm—at seventeen, weren't we all? Anyway, she dreams of living in a castle and has designs on that four-poster . . .'

We were interrupted by the waiter with the bill and, walking over to the car park afterwards, Fraser said: 'I was telling you about Morna—She's very artistic, has tremendous talent. If her mother hadn't died suddenly last year she would have gone to art school and studied design. She's very keen on interior decorating. However, her father has asthma and they're fairly poorly off, but he needs to live in the country for his health and, of course, being Morna, she insisted on staying at the garage and helping him. He had to retire early, as he was invalided out of the regular army several years ago. Salt of the earth is Morna'—he opened the car door for me—'a wonderful girl.'

As we drove off, I thought, a wonderful girl, and an artist who might specialise in interior decorating. With Fraser's flair for architecture, the future for them both—and for Deveron Castle—might hold out more promise than one first imagined. A most successful marriage aided by a highly skilled partnership.

'Perhaps you'd like to do a small detour and see what can happen to some of our castles.'

The two we inspected were ruined beyond hope of repair and Fraser said : 'As you'll notice in both these cases, there's a flourishing farm next door. This happened in the days when farmers found it expedient to take the stones from roofless castles to build dykes and stables and so forth, so much of the grandeur, the spiral staircases and turrets could often be traced to the piggery. There was no protection before the Ministry of Works decided to keep an eye on ancient monuments. I dare say the same might have happened at Deveron during the eighteenth and nineteenth centuries. However, the ruin hadn't set in then.'

He paused to negotiate a hump-backed bridge over a fast-moving torrent where dark and dangerous-looking rocks lay frighteningly far below. 'The ruin set in during Grandfather's day. He married the daughter of an earl and among many people who came to visit Deveron, lured on, I believe, by tales of her beauty, was Queen Victoria's son Bertie, when he was Prince of Wales. From all accounts the Deveron marriage had been a love match, but Grandmother grew tired of being a "bonnet laird's" lady, without a title and none of the social life she had known at her father's country seat in Kent. However, she desperately wanted to impress Bertie, especially when he became King Edward the Seventh, and as Grandfather had a hunting accident and spent most of his time in a wheelchair,

soon most of the treasures of Deveron began to disappear as she sold everything she could lay hands on
in order to keep up appearances and entertain the
royal household when they came to stay. His Majesty
must have been most impressed . . .'

I was dying to ask him if there was any truth in
Jeannie Deveron's hint that he had the 'blood royal'
and that his grandmother was really Bertie's
daughter, but I felt it would be rather tasteless.

'Anyway, when my father was a small boy she
eloped to London with one of the viscounts who came
up for shooting, and Deveron never saw her again.
Before there could be a scandal or divorce, he died.
Strangely enough, that piece of history repeated itself
exactly in my father's generation. My mother was
English, a wealthy landowner's daughter, and she too
soon tired of the life at Deveron, especially as impoverished was mild to describe the conditions by then.
She used to go to London twice a year, allegedly for
shopping and the theatre. One day she didn't return,
she'd met another man and father divorced her when
I was ten.'

'How sad for you.'

He shrugged. 'She made a dutiful appearance on
parents' day when I was at boarding-school, but I
haven't seen her since my father's funeral. I didn't
really want to, we had precious little to say to one
another and I suppose I was an unendearing little
monster blaming her for father's misfortunes. He spent
his last years crippled with arthritis—and with the
debt of Deveron hanging round his neck. I remember
as a child his struggles to cope with increasing dis-
ability and that was the reason why I wanted to do
something to make living easier for people who were
handicapped.'

He paused and added apologetically: 'Well, I started off talking about castles, didn't I? I hardly intended to bore you with the story of my unhappy life.' When I protested that I wasn't bored in the least, he smiled: 'If you could manage to stay for a day or two, I'd take you to Tillicross Castle which is owned by rich Americans. It's in much better state than those other two and I'm in process of restoring it for them.' He looked at his watch. 'Which reminds me—we'll have to rush. Morna and I have a dinner date there this evening. And the car has to go back this afternoon—they're short of small hiring-cars at present, and I didn't want a limousine type just to show you the sights.'

'You've been most kind. I do appreciate it.'

'Not at all—it seemed such a shame to have you come all this way and not inspect your native heath.'

Later, as we walked up the lane to the caravan, I said: 'Where do I stay tonight? You haven't forgotten, have you?'

Fraser frowned. 'You have a choice. You can sleep in the caravan here, it's very comfortable, I assure you —and I'll sleep in the castle. Or—the other way round. Am I to believe by the brightening of your eyes that you rather fancy the castle?'

'Please...'

He bowed. 'Your wish, ma'am, is my command. It's all been taken care of. I phoned Morna when we were at lunch and asked her to get Jeannie to prepare a little surprise for you.'

'Not the four-poster bed?' I asked excitedly.

He wagged a finger at me, suddenly a mischievous small boy. 'Now that would be telling and my lips are sealed. You'll have to go and find out for yourself, won't you?'

The sun had slid down behind the castle walls and left it, a great towering grey giant, far above us. Those walls looked as if neither sun nor happiness had ever touched them, they were made for sorrow and regret. Suddenly the hour seemed ominous and the coldness of premonition cast its shadow on a day that had been quite perfect.

What on earth was I doing electing to spend a night alone in this frightening fortress? When the door closed behind me I would be in a trap.

A trap.

And a solitary rook, homeward-bound, flopped on to the battlement and staring down at us cawed in shrilly triumph, as if to repeat the fatal words:

'Trap, trap . . . a trap . . .'

6

Fraser interpreted my anxious looks correctly, for he hurried into the caravan and emerged with a transistor radio which he thrust into my hand.

'Sure you really want to sleep over there—not scared, are you?' His smile was a challenge, defying me to say. Yes, I'm scared. I've changed my mind.

'Good girl. The radio will keep you company and . . .' he paused. 'You can have Rusty as companion to your vigil. She's a totally reliable guard dog and, what's more, will do whatever I tell her to.'

We were interrupted by the arrival of Morna's car.

Fraser introduced us and said: 'I'll dash upstairs and see that Jeannie has everything under control. No, no,' he added, as I made to accompany him. 'You stay here. Just wait patiently until everything's prepared for you.'

'Please don't be long,' said Morna, following his departure with an anxious sigh. Then, turning she smiled at me. 'I don't usually fuss, but Tillicross are sending a car for us. I thought I'd collect Fraser and save time. Did you have a pleasant day? I hope you enjoyed the castles of Strathdon?'

'I did indeed, although most I saw were in ruins.'

'Yes, it is rather depressing . . .'

In this setting her eyes looked quite normal, the odd luminosity had disappeared. I wondered if her eerie first appearance had been an illusion caused by the mist.

'. . . Get him to show you Tillicross. It's a perfect example of what can be done even to the most ruinous castle by restoration. He's very good at it, too.' She nodded in the direction of Deveron Castle's great bulk. 'It gives me great hopes that he isn't too late here. He does work so hard, it's only a question of money.'

I made sympathetic noises and she added: 'I do hope you approve of Fraser's idea—his surprise for you, I mean. I don't know whether it's a good idea, but it was the best that could be arranged at such short notice. Anyway, Jeannie's very efficient, as I expect you've discovered.'

'Her cooking's a dream.'

Morna smiled. 'Super. Anyway, it did seem a shame to have you go back to Yorkshire without spending the night in a genuine castle, especially as Fraser tells me you're related to the family.'

'Somewhat distantly, I'm afraid.'

'Oh, but so are we all—Jeannie too.' She looked at her watch. 'I hope you'll forgive our rough-and-ready attempts at Deveron hospitality.' She paused and looked anxiously down the lane. 'I do wish Fraser would hurry. What a man, he has absolutely no account of time—I expect he's decided to change despite Tillicross's informality.'

'I thought he was looking very elegant,' I said in his defence, remembering that feeling of closeness on the heather moor, and feeling rather guilty and somewhat annoyed for no good reason I could think of at that moment. I was going to say something sharp, then I noticed how, as she looked up at the castle again, her eyes were sad and tragic too—a pretty young face where the eyes did not quite belong, they were the eyes of someone who has suffered deeply and the marks of it remained. Strange that one so young should look so haunted and I realised that it was their expression only now that reminded me forcibly of our first encounter.

'I never had a chance to thank you properly for saving me from doing something idiotic when I was lost on Cairn Dever yesterday.'

She frowned. 'Doing something idiotic? I don't understand.'

'Well, you did show me the quick way down to Deveron Castle, didn't you?'

She looked at me quite unsmiling now. 'Oh yes, Fraser mentioned something about that,' she said slowly. 'I'm afraid you must have been mistaken, Miss Brent. You see, I've never been up Cairn Dever in my life. I would have been even more lost than you were.'

'But...' I began.

She made a swift small movement with her hand as

73

Fraser approached the car and I thought with quite unnecessary violence that her motive was: Don't let Fraser know.

What on earth was going on? Had I stumbled on to a village intrigue? Was she meeting some other man up Cairn Dever in the mist?

'I assure you it wasn't me,' she whispered and in a voice that changed completely for Fraser's benefit, she smiled and said: 'Enjoy your pleasant dreams. Everything all right, Fraser. Then do come along. We're late already.'

'Cheerio, then,' said Fraser with an apologetic grin. 'Stay with her, Rusty. Good girl, guard now.' And the astonishing dog moved to my side and sat determinedly close.

As I devoted my attention to patting her head, I was glad of an occupation, as I felt so angry with Morna I could barely say goodbye. I turned and saw Jeannie waiting at the castle door and marched after her up the spiral stairs to emerge in the Great Hall. Morna's behaviour probably had an innocent explanation, but it left a bad taste in my mouth, brought up as I had been by my father to the strictest honesty, where even the smallest of fibs was regarded as a punishable offence.

'You can tie a thief's hands, but you can't stop a liar's tongue from wagging,' Father would say.

I tried to thrust the unpleasantness of the last few minutes behind me as we emerged at what I remembered was the master bedroom. Opening the door, Jeannie said: 'This was the best I could manage at such short notice. I hope you won't examine the corners too closely.'

It was lovely—and I said so. The bed with plump white lace-trimmed pillows and its centuries-old brocade curtains, the matching bedspread, all embroidered by one of my ancestresses long ago. Lilacs bloomed in a deep vase and a fire burnt briskly in the old stone fireplace. But there was a stranger perfume than lilacs, the smell and touch of time itself, as if years of patchouli, of rose leaves, of wines and expensive tobaccos had seen their hour and left a fragment of themselves to linger for ever in bed-hangings and curtains.

'You'll need a fire. It gets chilly in the evenings, even in summer,' said Jeannie.

'Oh, thank you. It's so beautiful. I'm most grateful.'

'Across there, in what used to be the turret room, is a bathroom.' She gave me a kind smile from which every trace of her earlier hostility had vanished. 'Please look and see that there's everything you'll be needing.'

I did so, but when I came back to thank her again, she had gone, the door closed softly behind her.

Rusty swiftly claimed the rug in front of the fire as her own and stretched out full length, sighing in doggy content. I too wanted to sit by the fire and recapture a mood long past, to feel what it must have been like for my ancestors to have lived in this castle with servants, with all those gaunt empty rooms surrounding us, alive and occupied.

I found a programme of Sibelius on the transistor. Mrs. Deveron had left a lace-covered tray, there was coffee in a thermos jug, sandwiches and cake. I relaxed well content with my small cosy world, while outside the windows the spring day died in the storm which had threatened since morning, leaving me with a guilty feeling that somehow I had conjured it up with the brooding 6th Symphony. Yet strangely the storm, with its gale turning the leaves on the high trees

75

inside-out in its ferocity, intensified my own sensation of security that I was surrounded by a safe fortress, and I thought of the battles, storms and violence which had blown themselves out through the centuries, vanquished by these great walls.

Suddenly I wanted to keep these hours for ever, hold them in enchantment against the weary tide of unhappiness that had to be faced and lived through once I got back to Yorkshire. In a couple of days Deveron Castle would be a memory and I was grateful to Fraser for the dream-like quality of the time we had spent together.

He had all unknowing given me a time to lean against, indescribable and intangible. This precious episode would serve as safe anchorage in a future unimaginable except in monotones of grey, heightened here and there by the awful pain of seeing Ben marry Debbie and the dull emptiness of my life after that.

Perhaps in moments when it was unbearable I could remember this moment and be fortified by a freshness that never staled, a magic that never faded. Even the future of the castle itself, whether or not this room too would be a tumble of bricks and fallen masonry, with rooks nesting against an open sky, was a time that didn't belong to me. I had been given only this brief hour in Deveron's existence as my very own.

Suddenly I longed for Ben to share it with me. At that moment loving him was an overpowering sweetness as I wished that by some small miracle he would come here, find me and love me again. There was an addition to this fantasy now, a practicality which made such a day-dream worth while: That together we could help Fraser Deveron restore his castle and his glen.

However, even as I dreamed I was uncomfortably

aware that the role of philanthropist was never one to hang easily upon Ben Armstrong. It was too much at variance with the shrewd gleam, the light of calculation, the awareness of weak seams and threadbare velvet, that lay behind those beautiful eyes. Ben, alas, saw through most things—and all people. He cast a withering glance on lost causes. Only the sure, the almost certain, bets life offered were for him, lost causes he left to romantic idiots like me. And yet— everything he touched most surely turned to gold. Perhaps the glen, this castle—I hopefully rehearsed and discarded several speeches of persuasion . . .

At my feet Rusty stirred, whining, and moved swiftly to the door, snuffling, whimpering. The room was darker now and I realised I must have slept.

'Come in,' I called, expecting that Fraser had returned.

There was no answer. I called again, then opened the door. Looking down the corridor I was surprised to see Morna a few feet away. She was wearing a long hooded cape and her eyes had that strange luminosity of our first encounter. It was most effective and I wondered enviously where she bought her evening eye make-up.

She made a slight motion with her hand, indicating that I should follow her, and as I did so it was with further misgivings about why she so desperately wished to conceal our first meeting on Cairn Dever. My feminine intuition immediately suggested 'another man'. I hoped I was wrong, for Fraser seemed utterly devoted to her.

Suddenly I heard a whimper and, turning, there was Rusty sitting in the doorway I had just left.

'Come along, Rusty.' She made no attempt to follow me and lying down rested head on paws. With great supplicating eyes, she begged me to forgive her. 'Come along, lazybones, the exercise will do you good. Walkies, Rusty . . .' I snapped my fingers in vain. 'Oh, do come, you obstinate girl. You're supposed to look after me, remember?' I went back, put my hand on her collar and she shivered, gave another whimper. Then she drew back forcibly while feeble tail-wag plus reproachful doggy stare, plainly said: Please don't make me—I *will* come if you *absolutely* insist, but, please—I'd rather not.

I let go of her collar, thinking how odd it was. Morna stood a few yards away, waiting, but utterly detached. Earlier they'd made a great fuss of one another. I hoped Rusty wasn't ill.

'What shall I do?' I asked Morna, who continued to look merely bored. 'All right,' I said giving Rusty a push. 'Go back to your fire. I expect you're just bored to death, done it all so many times before, have you? I've never seen an animal so determined to get her own way,' I commented to Morna, who, obviously preoccupied by other things than Rusty's odd behaviour, urgently motioned that I should hurry.

As I followed her, Rusty watched, crying imploringly, stamping her paws as she begged me to stay. I could still hear her as we moved out of sight.

'Silly dog, does she often take bouts of temperament like that?' I asked the girl who walked silently ahead. 'How was the evening at Tillicross? You got back rather early, didn't you? Did you get caught in the storm? It was quite wild here. I listened to a super concert. Thanks for arranging the bedroom back there —I do appreciate it, and I'm really looking forward to sleeping in my four-poster . . .'

But my determined efforts at light conversation went quite unheeded and I wondered uneasily if she were a little deaf, for not only had she ignored all my questions but gave no indication that she listened—or heard. I had the sudden brilliant idea that partial deafness would also explain the intensity of her stare. Otherwise, her behaviour was rather inexplicable.

Suddenly I had other problems. I was out of breath. The reason was that no matter how I hurried to keep up with her, to reach her side, she always remained those few paces ahead.

'Hold on—what's all the hurry?' I asked. She stopped momentarily without looking back, but after that occasionally hesitated, as if to make sure I didn't get lost in the maze of corridors which had absorbed us once we crossed the Great Hall.

Now I understood the reason for Rusty's lack of interest in our excursion. The temperature had fallen and the light diminished, diluted through stained-glass windows with heraldic designs, birds, beasts and flowers, added to the natural gloom and claustropho-bia of wood-panelled corridors little more than a yard wide. Morna's shoes were soundless and I was conscious of the echo of my own footsteps in the heavy silence, the only sound but for the sad and tearful frenzy of raindrops hurled against glass.

I shivered with a sudden longing for the room I had left with its cheerful fire. 'I hope you know the way back,' I said cheerfully. 'Fraser tells me it's very easy to get lost here and wander about for hours. Not something I'd care to contemplate in this light.'

And I meant it. For the eerie atmosphere was more than disuse, mustiness and the coloured light from the windows. Had I been susceptible to such impressions I would have admitted to an overpowering conscious-ness of times past. The past with its people were no longer dead and laid to dust, they were alive, running parallel with us. And only a gossamer veil, the blink of an eyelid, separated us from the vast chasm of eternity itself.

At last Morna stopped at one of the narrow strips of panelling. The only illumination in the gloom had been through the coloured window. Now, as my eyes grew accustomed to the lack of light, I realised there was also light *behind* the panel. Morna had, quite unnoticed by me, opened a door which fitted snugly into it.

'How marvellous. An original Alexander Deveron, I presume.' I followed her inside. 'Fraser told me he had a great sense of humour, designing the maze pattern—but a secret room too? Fraser didn't mention this.'

The room was small and square, lit by a tiny slit window in a very thick wall. I sniffed the air. A strong smell of damp, disuse and decay, bottled up over many decades. From the gloom appeared shapes of furniture. Table, chair and an ancient curtained bed. I went over and inspected it—then I shrank back in horror, for its curtains melted at my touch. They were of gossamer, made by the cobwebs and accumulated dust of centuries.

So this was Fraser's surprise. Curiously enough, I wouldn't have expected that he would have entrusted this particular practical joke to a third person. He was such a romantic, I could have imagined him wanting to bring any visitor here himself, to show off another facet of Alexander Deveron's genius.

And deciding that Morna too concealed a sense of humour under her shyness, I concealed my revulsion as best I could and said: 'All quite fascinating. Thanks for bringing me to see it, but I wouldn't want to sleep here. I suppose I did ask for it, going on about ambitions to sleep in an ancient bed.'

Turning to walk out with some dignity, I found that Morna had already gone. What was much worse, the door through which we had entered had closed behind her. The *pièce de résistance* in the grim joke was the fact that the door was so well hidden as to blend perfectly into the other panels, nor was there any handle or visible sign of what might open it. I ran my hands down the closed seams of wood.

Then slowly my scalp began to rise. There was nothing. I was trapped in a room without a door. And even as the feeling of terror and suffocation mounted, I knew I was not alone. The room had another silent occupant.

Sufficient light remained to illuminate a pale face, a shadowy outline of someone standing by the far wall.

There was someone else—someone waiting . . .

7

Someone waiting . . .

A silent motionless figure, eyes bright in the gloom.

Seconds later, relief flooded over me as I realised I was face-to-face with a life-sized oil-painting. Of Morna, strangely enough, although the light was too poor to see clearly. I steered it towards the scant light from the narrow window.

Morna. And it must have been painted by Fraser, for I guessed that like most architects he probably dabbled in painting at some time. She held something in her hand. A white rose. Fraser had painted her as the White Rose of Deveron, the Jacobite heroine Great-Uncle had told me about, who sheltered Prince Charles after Culloden and was killed by the English Redcoats.

As I settled the painting back in its corner, I wished the light was better. For an amateur it suggested an excellent effort, although a little outdated in composition. I wondered how Fraser had managed the tiny hair-cracks in the canvas which added a remarkable effect of antiquity. Perhaps his materials had been sadly at fault, through lack of funds to buy the best, and that was why he had banished it to this room.

I looked around, shivering, wishing Morna would return and release me from what was rapidly taking on dimensions of a prison. Practical joking was one thing, but now the incident had its grim aspect. Geese were not walking over my grave at that moment, but whole gaggles of them were walking up and down my spine in a very determined and terrifying manner.

I tapped on the panel where I imagined the door was. 'Morna, Morna. There's no handle on this side. Let me out, will you?'

I didn't really expect an answer, nor that the door would swing open at my command. A moment later I was hammering on the panel, afraid now with more than the cold and the silence that surrounded me.

A frightening thought—why was Morna pretending to be the White Rose of Deveron and trying to terrify me out of my wits with a secret room—a room without any door? Had she used this deception before in fact—on Cairn Dever to direct me through the mist to Deveron Castle—and safety? In that instance, a harmless imposture—was the explanation simple, that she was still enough of a child to take pleasure in a game of make-believe?

I dare not think deeper—then. Speculation, the germ of an idea too monstrous to entertain sanely, I pushed back into the recess of absurdity where it belonged, refusing to recognise anything but the obvious: that Morna, for some obscure reason, resented my presence and was trying to scare me away, was going to elaborate and ingenious lengths to accomplish this feat.

And what else could be the reason but female jealousy? In her own way she was teaching me a lesson, adoring Fraser and imagining with a child's lack of logic that I was trying to lure him away from her. Of course, this didn't quite explain why she should try to *save* me on the mountain, except that I was still a stranger then. I had no connection with Fraser at that time, as far as she knew.

Not altogether happy with this rather shaky explanation, I tried to examine my surroundings without hysteria. I must find a way out. Running my hands over the panelling revealed no secret lock and I could still see perfectly where the door fitted neatly into its frame, a masterpiece of work by Alexander Deveron, the castle's first laird, that wizard of sixteenth-century gimmickry. I wonder if Fraser who had apparently inherited his flair for architecture from this ancestor also appreciated the hidden room. I only wished he was around to show me how to escape.

I was beginning to panic, for the room was growing gloomier and more indistinct as day faded through the narrow window. Quite frankly, I didn't relish the prospect of being locked in here for the night. There were other hazards to be faced—once out of the room I still had to negotiate the labyrinth of corridors outside. It was imperative I escape before darkness fell.

'Morna—Morna,' I called again, but without any hope that she was still there.

With a feeling of revulsion I examined my surroundings closely. All this set from a horror film lacked were the bleached bones of some forgotten prisoner. Suddenly I noticed an old carved chest and, expecting signs of violence or forgotten crime in its depths, I nervously opened the lid, which creaked with blood-curdling promptitude. Its depths mercifully were empty of all but a few alarmed spiders weaving webs with less alacrity than they had shown on the little bed with its ghoulish drapes. In a complete absence of corpses, I decided that the hidden room had been priest's hole rather than prison cell.

Standing on tiptoe, I looked through the narrow slit of window to where a dark fir forest marched up a steep slope. There was no sign of human habitation on this deserted side of the castle and I guessed I could stay here for ever and never attract anyone's attention. Unless Morna had a change of heart, when she thought I had learned my lesson, whatever that mysterious lesson might be. And I didn't relish the prospect that I was dealing with some form of emotional instability, despite her gentle appearance.

Fighting back panic, the need to scream, to go to pieces, methodically I searched the room. My teeth positively chattered with cold—and terror, as added to such natural fears of being incarcerated, starved to a slow death or going mad, another horror grew deep in my mind that I dared neither name nor contemplate in these surroundings. The terror of the unknown, added to the natural, the supernatural. Something about that picture that I was refusing fully to recognise . . .

In the world of Aynley House, of Perseus Plastics, the nearest I had come to any psychic experience was a teenage passion for morbid stories, for ghoul and ghost. There was a sameness, a predictability about such superimposed horrors, the clanking chains and spectral figures. Then one day I discovered Henry James and all spooky stories became laughable by comparison with the understatement, the implied horrors of *The Turn of the Screw.*

It gave me little satisfaction to find at this moment that none of my early fictional excursions into such realms had scared me more than the silence of my cobwebbed prison and Morna's strange deception.

Deception? queried the part of my brain busily at work, sifting, sorting, putting explanation and experience through its own highly efficient computer. Deception? Of course, said the part where logic lay. What else could it be but deception? After all, Morna shepherding me through the corridors had been as real as Fraser or Mrs. Deveron. *But what about the picture —what about the White Rose?*

'No,' I said aloud. 'No! Why shouldn't Fraser paint Morna as the White Rose?' A romantic gesture, nothing more.

And stifling fears monstrously growing every moment, my patient search was rewarded. A dismal corner cupboard which I opened and found empty at first glance. But when I ran my hands across its back panel it revealed a latched door which led out through the panelling on to one of the spiral staircases I had noticed at regular junctions along the corridors. To anyone looking in casually, this double door would appear to be only a cupboard; another piece of Alexander Deveron's ingenuity, one last bastion of escape.

Thankful to be free, I ran swiftly down the dark twisting stairs when suddenly before me a flash of wings, and a rook, full of wrathful indignation, rose screaming from its nest at my feet. The rush of air, the bird's flight, brought me to a full stop.

Two steps further and the stairs ended in thin air. The bird had saved my life. Below in the dim light was tangled vegetation, through which gleamed the pavement of an old terrace. Sickeningly far below.

'Help,' I called. 'Help!' But the now thoroughly disturbed and irate rookery drowned all other sounds. Wearily I turned and climbed the stairs again to where it emerged at the end of a long narrow corridor. I couldn't be sure that this was the one which concealed the secret room without knowing how many floors I had descended in my flight down the spiral stairs.

The corridor led at right angles into another corridor which in its turn led at right angles into another . . .

Despite the cold, my forehead was beaded with sweat. I must risk the darkness, stop and think. After all, the castle was in partial ruin. I had suffered enough horrors this evening and even free from my prison I had only exchanged it for other unseen dangers. Steps leading nowhere could turn into floors that gave way, trapdoors—some inspired by Alexander Deveron's ingenuity and some mere tributes to time's decay. I couldn't afford to take chances in this castle which by night might well assume the monstrous terrors of a funfair House that Jack Built.

At the angle of the next corridor I stopped and visualised my journey with Morna. Which way had we turned? Left—I was sure it was always left. If, then, the pattern obeyed the basically simple rules of most complicated mazes, the key lay in always returning in the reverse direction.

Right. I would keep turning right—and I would pray!

The next four corridors ended in angled turns and, sure that I was hopelessly lost, to my joy I saw the Great Hall ahead. After that it was an easy matter to find the master bedroom where Rusty waited, greeting me with relief as hysterical as my own. Her concern was very touching after all I had been through. She even cried a little—and so did I.

However, I was soon fortified by more coffee and biscuits, shared by a fully restored Rusty, effusively showing her delight with much tail-banging and head thrusting into my lap.

As I drank the last of the coffee I felt I had never been so tired before and I hardly remember tumbling into bed. I slept immediately and for a moment when I opened my eyes next morning I enjoyed to the full the luxury of waking in a four-poster bed in surroundings that seemed not at all strange. I sat up, relishing the romance of it all, the chance that had led me to Deveron. I saw myself telling Ben and Rona about it, bragging a little because they had wealth but they didn't have a real live castle, a trifle ruined but very much still alive, in their family history. All they had were some very nasty Border sheep-stealers and rapists.

Rapists—then I remembered what I had dreamed.

A terrifying dream, so vivid I could scarcely believe it was not real and I could still sicken at the memory of it. I was the White Rose, running up Cairn Dever, wearing men's clothes—my prince's borrowed clothes —pretending to be him, luring the Redcoats away from Deveron Castle while he took the path across the glen where loyal men with fast horses waited to take him to safety. Although in my dream I was used to

Cairn Dever in all its different moods, now I felt both mountain and the mist, that should have been my friends, were enemies. I couldn't explain why, knowing every inch of the path I took, I should have any doubt that I could give the soldiers the slip.

I had a good start on my pursuers, stopping occasionally for breath, wishing I could discard heavy cloak and man's hat. That was the worst experience, trying to keep it on my head. Even with my hair stuffed into it, it was sizes too big and every now and again, locks of my own hair became dislodged streaming over my shoulders, hurtling into my eyes. Even my hair was an enemy this day.

Then the worst—or almost the worst—that could happen, did. The mist lifted suddenly so that when I stopped I saw only a hundred yards away a line of Redcoats making their way up the hill. I must have been clearly outlined, for there was a shout of triumph as they saw me. I turned, ran upwards, ever upwards, their musket-shots falling wide.

I could still beat them. Nothing could touch me.

Then it happened. I was thrown to the ground, I heard the roar of noise, the searing pain as a bullet crashed into my shoulder. I staggered, fell, wanting to drift away on a tide of pain too great too bear. Perhaps for a moment I fainted. Then looking up, hearing my pursuers nearer, I saw the shrine.

For some reason I believed it could save me. Stumbling, I reached it, fell on my knees and, making the sign of the cross, I whispered :

'Mary, Mother of God, I have sinned . . . In this hour of my death, deliver me . . .'

She seemed to smile, clutching her Baby. There was so much peace with them both. Then I heard the noise behind me, turned, saw the sweating faces of the soldiers. I heard their laughter, their obscenities as they dragged me from the shrine. I heard the tearing of cloth as they pulled the clothes off me as easily as petals from a flower. But I think I was already dead before the rest happened . . .

Sometime it was over and I was out of myself, watching from a little distance away. I saw what had been me lying motionless, fair hair streaming in a pool of blood. I saw their bayonets rise, crash down, rise again red. I turned my head away and looked down at my buckled shoes. My feet were wet and I was cold, cold with the ill-wind that blew through the heather, keening for a girl who had met such a death without uttering a single cry.

And at that moment I opened my eyes. The gentle ticking of my watch on the bedside table was reassuring evidence that I was Candida Deveron Brent, living in the twentieth century, and all I had seen and suffered was as audience at some monstrous nightmare. It was five o'clock, but still what I had seen, who I had been in those terrible moments, were slow to fade. Tossing restlessly, sure that further sleep was impossible, I went to the bathroom and, returning with a glass of water, glanced out of the bedroom window.

There, far below, all was quietly normal, the Murder Field only a piece of untidy waste land, with boulders and heather growing all awry. Deveron certainly had an astonishing effect on my imagination—a family massacre one night, a murder the next. I was about to return to bed when I noticed a figure walking up the lane, carrying what looked like a spade over his shoulder. It was Fraser. What an odd time of the morning—what could he be digging for—and where?

After such a crowded night it wasn't surprising that

I had dressed and prepared to go downstairs and have breakfast with Fraser in the caravan as we had arranged, when I remembered that other dream—about a cobwebbed bed, a locked room and a picture.

Except that it was no dream . . .

Furiously I rushed to the door, threw it open. I half-expected to see Morna lurking there, amused at my distress. But the corridor, a dismal place even in broad daylight, was empty. Rusty stared at me amazed, as furiously I banged the door and marched angrily through the Great Hall.

I was livid. I'd certainly tell Fraser what I thought of the 'surprise' he had promised me. As for Morna, his most willing accomplice—I would give her and her practical jokes a piece of my mind. If jealousy were the root cause, I would make it abundantly clear that she could keep Fraser Deveron. I certainly didn't want him.

Rusty, obviously attuned to the vagaries of human moods, walked cautiously well to heel, anxious to please and trying to meanwhile look insignificant in the hope that she would be overlooked when my rage exploded.

I heard laughter inside the caravan and opened the door without knocking. Morna and Fraser were seated at the table and my heart only momentarily softened at the delicious smell of bacon frying on the stove. Their heads were together and they were enjoying a huge joke. Only it took scant imagination to guess that my gullibility—that jolly episode in the room without a door—was the subject of their mirth.

Fraser greeted me politely, while Morna, still smiling, popped bread into the electric toaster beside her. 'Did you sleep well?' asked Fraser, hurrying over to attend to the frying bacon. And quite unaware of my furious countenance they both continued to look very pleased with themselves.

'Eventually,' I said grimly.

'Stay a little longer,' said Fraser idly. 'It's always difficult to sleep in a strange bed. I assure you it's very comfortable when you get used to it. Curtains didn't put you off, did they? Too bad if you were claustrophobic,' he added tackling the contents of the pan with a fork.

Morna, pouring coffee into three mugs, smiled gently. 'I hope the bed was warm enough for you. It was a good idea to get Jeannie to light that fire, Fraser. There's something charming about going to sleep in firelight, don't you think so?'

He nodded. 'That room can be so cold, even in high summer.'

'But not quite as cold, you must admit, as the other room Morna so kindly offered me.'

She frowned, looking puzzled—and innocent too.

'I presume you hadn't realised there was no handle on my side of the door—that it only opens from the corridor.'

I decided that she must be a considerable actress, for her face was absolutely blank and the glances she and Fraser exchanged clearly indicated that I had gone crazy.

Fraser came over leaned on the table. 'What's all this about a room without a door?' he asked gently, humouring me.

'Oh, haven't you told him?' I asked Morna. 'Is he not in the secret? Well, well, I did think the joke would be too good not to share.'

'Joke?' asked Morna. 'What joke? I don't understand.'

'Oh, come along now, I think you do understand.

Look, I have as much sense of humour as anyone, but the game's up. Let's all put our cards on the table and then we can all have a good laugh—at my expense. I admit it, I *was* pretty dim. Of course, I appreciated sleeping in the master bedroom and, I admit, I was a bit brash drooling over four-poster beds and suchlike. In my somewhat naive fashion, I suppose I was begging to have that kind of trick played on me . . .'

'What kind of trick?' asked Fraser. He wasn't laughing now.

'Oh, being locked in that secret room in the corridor,' I said casually, 'your favourite practical joking point for visitors, the room with the bed and those fetching cobwebbed curtains. You know . . .'

'I don't know, otherwise I wouldn't be asking,' said Fraser coldly. 'Now then, shall we start again?'

'Again?'

'Yes. My dear girl, I haven't a clue what you're talking about.'

'You will have, when Morna explains.'

Fraser gave her a questioning look, but she shrugged helplessly. 'All right, let's hear your account, Candida,' he said.

I laughed. 'Well, there isn't much to tell you—you both know the story a lot better than I do. Surely it was all carefully arranged that when you got back from Tillicross, Morna should mysteriously conduct me to the secret room . . .'

'There isn't any secret room that I know of,' Fraser interrupted. 'And what is more, it certainly wasn't Morna who conducted you there.'

'Of course it was, even if she was pretending to be the White Rose—there's nothing wrong with my eyesight. Oh, come on, now, you two—admit it, and we'll all have a good laugh.'

'What time was this?'

'About nine.'

'At that time we were having coffee.' Fraser looked across at Morna, who with downcast eyes had listened to my accusation with an expressionless face. In fact, far from the guilty smiles I expected Fraser looked merely annoyed.

I tried again. 'You are rather splendid on alibis, you two. First Morna directs me down Cairn Dever to Deveron—while you swear she was at the garage all the time. Then she locks me in a room and is conveniently having dinner with you . . .'

'I must go,' said Morna hurriedly, pulling at Fraser's sleeve. 'I promised Father. I really must go.' She gave me an anguished glance.

Without looking at her, Fraser said: 'All right, Morna. Wait for me in the car.' He turned back to me. 'This won't take long,' he added grimly.

Morna shrugged, a gesture that indicated a bewildered apology. 'I wish I knew what you were talking about, Miss Brent. I'm sorry you think I'm playing tricks on you—I'm afraid you've got it all wrong somewhere . . .'

'Don't you bother about her, Morna,' said Fraser sharply, 'I'll sort it out,' and with a furious look in my direction, he took her arm gently and shepherded her out of the caravan.

'Please don't be long,' I heard her whisper.

He bounded inside and I was ready for him. 'You must think I'm a fool . . .'

He leaned across the table. 'I don't think you're a fool. I *do* think, however, that you're suffering from a brainstorm, or some sort of hallucination.' He paused. 'Otherwise I don't think you could be so monstrously cruel to Morna.'

'Cruel? I like that. Why should I be cruel? I'm the one who's been tricked. I'll have you know she nearly scared me out of my wits. Locking me in a room without a door. I suppose you imagine there's nothing cruel about that. After all, I only asked to sleep in a four-poster—I didn't bargain for this cobwebbed creation out of Dracula. And you call *me* cruel . . .'

'Yes, I do. Come over here.' Taking my arm, he thrust me towards the window. 'Look.'

Morna was walking slowly to her car, if that was what her progress could be called. She limped badly, as if one leg was considerably shorter than the other.

I turned to Fraser : 'When did she do that?'

'She didn't do anything. She had polio when she was two and has been lame ever since. Why do you suppose she always wears trousers, long capes? If you use your eyes next time you'll also observe that she wears a caliper on her left leg. Anyway, even if she hadn't been with me last night, I would still believe her word. I've known and loved Morna since she was a little girl. I can assure you that practical jokes are utterly alien to her nature. She hasn't an ounce of cruelty or malice in her, despite the fate that might have soured a less-warm heart.'

She had reached the car and was leaning against it, waiting for Fraser. 'Of course, she can drive that special car with its automatic gears, but she has never climbed Cairn Dever, where you allege you first met her. She is hardly capable of walking any distance, of climbing stairs, let alone a mountain. She can heave herself upstairs by a handrail, but the only time she has ever been up the spiral staircase in the castle was when I carried her there four years ago. She has never been inside alone in her life.'

94

8

For a moment, as Morna heaved herself awkwardly into the car, I caught a glimpse of caliper and of withered leg. My heart ached with compassion that one so young and otherwise perfectly made should be so marred. My next feeling was of revulsion. Against myself, combined with a longing that the earth would open and swallow me, that my terrible words of accusation could be unsaid, words that still hung like a glass barrier in the silence between Fraser and me.

Then, outside, a car horn, urgent, insistent, as Morna waited for Fraser to join her.

'I am telling the truth,' I said, trying to reach the stony-faced man who stood at my side in the caravan. 'I didn't know Morna was crippled. Surely you know I'm horrified by what I said, I wouldn't have hurt her for anything.' The silence remained. 'You must believe me. I was mistaken, but if it wasn't Morna yesterday, then it was her double I met . . .'

He swept aside my clumsy attempt at explanation. 'Sorry, Candida, but I have to go now. Finish your breakfast. Amuse yourself until lunchtime, then we'll talk about it,' he added with a forced smile.

Not if I can help it, I thought, watching him jump into the passenger seat beside Morna, with Rusty, all oblivious of the human drama, leaping joyously behind them. Morna was obviously upset, for with his arm around her Fraser spoke urgently, imploringly. She nodded listlessly, her profile tragic, remote.

I turned away, feeling sick. I could guess what he was saying, hear him apologising for my appallingly

95

cruel behaviour. No, Fraser Deveron, you won't see me again, not if I can help it.

How could I ever face them? Added to embarrassment was also indignation, the sense of injustice and betrayal. Somehow I had been the victim of a hideous trick by which they believed I lied and I was helpless to convince them otherwise. There was another feeling too. Sadness that I would never see Fraser or his glen again, and that my wild hope of persuading Ben Armstrong to help Fraser make that impossible dream for Deveron come true was also doomed.

Quickly gathering my things together, I walked down the lane, thankful that I didn't meet anyone and that Jeannie's cottage was deserted, her door closed. I shivered. This was a strange uneasy world I had briefly encountered, where too many questions remained unanswered, too many loose ends unexplained. Right at the beginning there was that extraordinary business of the Murder Field, peaceful now in a morning haze of sunshine. Just an untidy sprawl of boulders and heather, where an occasional stunted tree forlorn against a tenacious existence was the only living thing that fought for survival.

I blinked against the sun. Could I possibly have heard the noise of that long-ago massacre, the ghostly cries and shots—or was hallucination, decently dismissed as nightmare, already here with me on that first night I stayed in Deveron? A few hours before I had encountered Morna's double in broad daylight— or, more appropriately, thick mist on Cairn Dever. The same girl who had summoned me to a rendezvous in a secret room in Deveron Castle and had subsequently haunted my dreams in the guise of the White Rose of Deveron, as I watched her wounded and slain by the Redcoat soldiers after Prince Charles Edward

Stuart's escape from Culloden more than two hundred years ago.

Now, as I waited at the bus-stop, there was nothing but peace in Deveron. The sun gleamed on what looked like the harmless green slopes of Cairn Dever, with promise of fair weather. It was only when I looked closer that I realised the patches of white were murderous corries still filled with snow. Somewhere up there lay, dead and unburied, Great-Uncle Jamie the shepherd. I shivered, then remembered that when they removed the snow from him it would be no shocking sight of decomposition but merely as if he had died yesterday, perhaps in the dignified illusion, the harmless eccentricity, that he was the grandiose laird of Deveron.

How he must have disapproved of the unpretentiousness of young Fraser Deveron, who regarded himself as merely a farmer with rather more unproductive land than he could manage.

I hoped they wouldn't expect me to come back for my great-uncle's funeral. Perhaps Ben would come in my place. He adored formal occasions, the opportunity of making new business contacts that even funerals offered. And the opportunity of making rather long speeches, too, I thought uncharitably.

I took a deep breath, savouring the beauty before me, as if to fill my heart for ever with Deveron as I would remember it. With trees brightly budded in spring radiance of bridal greens and whites, the birds singing their symphony of passionate rapture into the wine-clear air, the dappled lane soft-moving in sun and shade.

Goodbye, Deveron.

Whatever had happened to me during my stay would remain a mystery. Suddenly it was no longer important even to have a solution, for once I was back at Perseus Plastics all this would dissolve into the unreality of some long-past dream. One thing was certain. Neither Ben nor his mother Rona would believe a single word of my incredible tale. Down-to-earth, practical, sceptical people, they would, of course, listen to it with polite smiles, but if I watched carefully I would find them exchanging secret glances, denoting in the code of their shared intimacy I had never broken : 'Another of Candida's wild imaginings. How she does go on.'

And I wondered, jealous again, were they perhaps relieved to find that Debbie from America was exactly like themselves and if that was why Ben had fallen in love with her?

At the very last moment, as the yellow bus trundled slowly round the corner, I looked quickly towards the castle, remembering with a sense of unbelievable loss how Fraser had come yesterday morning in time to stop me taking this bus. I remembered too how we had shared a prospect of hills afterwards in an enchanted glen with ruined castles, a golden eagle's flight and Rusty's quiver of excitement at the dog-fox's warning bark.

The bus stopped before me. As I climbed aboard, for an instant I wished I had less stubborn pride and could have borne to wait in the caravan for Fraser's return. Well, I would never get another chance now. Already the lane had disappeared and most of the long road back to Deveron village. The point of no return was past and slinging my suitcase on to the rack I sat nevertheless close to the window, trying to keep Cairn Dever in my sights as long as possible and wondering if Fraser would perhaps know an instant's sadness, too, when he returned and found me gone. I would never know.

If I had a mind for enjoying scenery, the journey back to Muldoune Bridge was breath-taking. But in some strange way I found it obliterating all that had happened since my arrival, like some film moving backwards, returning me to the point in time where it all began. Suddenly I felt with a dull ache that I was suspended in a void where not even the present belonged to Candida Brent. The magnificent landscape was remote and unreal. It seemed impossible that the houses, large and small, croft and mansion, could be occupied by real people, that behind those walls dwarfed by distance a baby might be coming into the world, or an old man dying, or two lovers in a fever against time were asleep in each other's arms. As for the fat fluffy brown hens, the shaggy brown Highland cattle, they were animated cartoon creatures painted on a backdrop, the figments of imagination.

As the miles vanished, I longed to stay in this fantasy world, knowing that ahead and inescapable awaited the solid miseries of Ben and his new love. When the bus stopped for its ten-minute break outside the woollen mill where I had bought him the elegant sweater that had been the beginnings of all my troubles with Deveron, I found the doors locked. I thought of my wallet reposing still among the sealskin purses and my inability to find someone to retrieve it felt like a personal conspiracy on the part of the absent owners.

I received a confirmation of my fears from the only shop open, a small general store already doing a fine trade in sweets and ice-cream.

'This is the spring holiday weekend. They'll no' be open until tomorrow.'

So Fraser had warned me. Had I not been so distrustful, I could have saved myself another disappointment. No matter. Having come this far and spent only a fraction of Fraser's loaned five pounds on my bus fare, I was now determined to head on back to Aberdeen on the second stage of my journey to York. I would get the station-master to phone Ben at Perseus Plastics, if he didn't believe my story of the missing wallet. They would certainly believe Ben Armstrong.

Appeasing hunger with an ice-cream cone instead of the delicious breakfast I had scorned at Deveron, I caught sight of a very unremarkable reflection. Chestnut-brown hair, green eyes in a pale face with high cheekbones. I studied it ruefully. Even when I spoke the truth, no one believed me. Did I indeed have the unmistakable markings of a criminal type? Was there something shifty about my expression that made people instinctively disbelieve me? Truthfulness had been bred in me and yet I wasn't believed. And that did hurt.

Licking my ice-cream absently and with little enjoyment, I made my way back to the bus where other passengers, similarly employed, suddenly dispersed inside. The immediate landscape was occupied by two figures.

A few yards away, striding purposefully in my direction was a young man with striking red hair and, by his side, a long-legged Irish setter. Fraser and Rusty.

For a second I thought they hadn't spotted me and looked around, frantic for some means of escape. There wasn't one. Neither an open shop nor doorway into which I could dart. Already it was too late, for Rusty's howl of delight at my approach could have been heard almost back to Deveron.

'I came to see if the mill was open.'

'You could have saved yourself the journey, if you'd

listened. I told you they were closed until Tuesday,' replied Fraser, without even the vestige of a smile. 'I suppose your suitcase is in the bus there.'

'Yes. When I had come this far I decided I might as well keep going.' I paused lamely as he watched me with a sour expression. 'There seemed little point in staying.'

'Really?' he asked me mockingly, hands on hips. 'Really? One might have imagined with some small justification that you owed me—not to mention Morna—some explanation for your extraordinary behaviour this morning.'

Behind us the conductress had rejoined the bus, pressed the bell. The engine sprang to life.

'You didn't believe my story,' I said sullenly, 'so what was the point of labouring explanations.'

He took my arm in a firm grasp. 'I hadn't time to listen this morning, Morna's father had an urgent appointment and I wanted a lift over here. It was hardly an opportune moment to give your story the full attention it undoubtedly needs,' he added sarcastically. 'Now I have time. Go on, get in. You'll miss your bus. Oh, don't worry, I'm coming with you . . .'

As I took my place, he sat down firmly beside me, cutting off all hope of escape. As the bus drove off we must have presented an intriguing prospect. My indignation, my *sotto voce* protests doubtless indicating a lovers' quarrel at full tilt to the passengers in the adjacent seats, who stared ahead in the unnatural attitudes of people pretending to be invisible while anxious not to miss a single word. Even Rusty's sigh as she lay down and rested her head on her paws, occupying a good deal of passageway as she did so, suggested clearly that between her beloved humans such scenes took place with boring regularity.

I gave up protesting. I couldn't stop him travelling beside me, but I needn't speak to him. Mutinously I edged as close to the window as possible and turning my head examined the passing landscape with exaggerated interest. Fraser gave up his attempts at communication and relapsed into sullen silence. When at last he stood up I thought I had won. He was going to leave the bus—and me, thank goodness—in peace.

He reached up for my suitcase and removed it from the rack. 'Right,' he said, taking hold of my arm. 'Come along, this is our stop—dear,' he added for the benefit of the passengers.

'Tillicross, sir?' asked the conductress, restraining her amusement.

'I'm not coming,' I told him. 'Put back my case.'

He shook his head. I sprang to my feet and struggled to gain possession of it. 'I'll take that—hurry now, we mustn't keep the children waiting. Remember it's almost time you fed the twins, darling,' he said loudly, and beaming at the intrigued faces around us he marched me firmly down the passage and out of the bus, wishing the conductress a hearty good-day. By the roadside he watched the bus vanish and then released his firm grip on my arm.

'Oh no.' I stamped my foot angrily. 'This is too much. You can't keep me here against my will.' I leaned my suitcase against the fence. 'For your information, I intend waiting here until the next bus arrives—and the twins can starve to death—dear—for all I care.'

'Tut, tut, I consider that most unfeeling of you.'

'And I consider your so-called sense of humour most unfunny. You made us look like a pair of prize idiots.'

'You might help matters by not behaving like one in the first place. Oh, I'm sorry, Candida, but you are

102

the most stubborn, truculent girl I have ever met.'

'Compared with you, *I* don't even begin to be stubborn. Now would you please leave me alone—and that goes for you too, dog,' I added tearfully to Rusty, who was nosing at my hand and making imploring sounds as if to remind me that I hadn't made a fuss of her for some time.

'That's enough, Rusty,' said Fraser firmly, and sighed. 'Well, I suppose I can't stop you leaving—by the way, that's Tillicross up the lane.'

I gave it a jaundiced glance. 'How splendid—another castle, just what I have always wanted. Except that I'm not in the mood for a conducted tour today. Thank you very much, but I've had castles up to my ears.'

'This isn't a tour. I specially wanted you to see Tillicross. I'm sorry I bored you yesterday,' he added in wounded tones. 'I wouldn't have gone on so long, but you did give every indication of enthusiasm.'

I felt like adding: Too much evidently and that was doubtless the reason for the practical joke with the secret room without a door. But the words stuck and I said instead: 'That was yesterday. Goodbye, Fraser,' and, turning on my heel, I started to walk away.

The next moment I was rudely dragged back to face him. Luckily we had the road and this entire piece of the world to ourselves at that moment, with no one except Rusty—who had flopped down with a yawn—to witness Fraser with his red hair, his belligerent face, struggling with a suitcase and a girl equally determined to have her own way. Quite suddenly I was again reminded of that resemblance I had imagined on our first encounter—Fraser Deveron as Robert the Bruce.

'All you need is a two-handed sword,' I said angrily.

He stared down into my face. 'I don't usually smack girls, but, believe me, at this moment the temptation is overwhelming. All right, have your own way,' and he released my arm.

In the silence that followed I looked with regret at the handsome building which occupied the skyline at the top of the lane. Had I found it in different circumstances, I would have been overjoyed, delighted to be taken on what I had so scathingly dismissed as 'another tour'.

Fraser found my hand and held my fingers tight. 'Please, Candida, don't let's argue any more.' His voice was kind, he smiled and the result was enchanting. 'Do come to Tillicross with me.'

'Very well,' I said stiffly. 'A truce.'

And his sixteenth-century ancestor, Alexander who built Deveron Castle, could not have bowed lower or in more courtly fashion over my hand as he raised it to his lips.

'A truce it is, then,' he said softly.

9

'Tillicross is a much smaller castle than Deveron,' said Fraser, as we walked up the lane. 'It was intended for peaceful domesticity, with just enough defence to deter predatory neighbours—and any warring clansmen who might be returning empty-handed and rather disgruntled from some Highland foray.'

I followed him through a stone archway into a tiny courtyard. Above a fine arched door, a handsome window stared down on a peaceful scene of trees in tubs, a well, which Fraser declared: 'Purely ornamental now, of course,' and rang the doorbell.

He waited, rang a second time and then turned the handle and whispered, 'In you go.' As he closed the door behind us, I hesitated.

'There is someone at home.' I seized his arm. 'Wait, Fraser, we can't just rush in. Maybe the doorbell doesn't work—how about giving it another ring?'

He laughed at my shocked expression and said, 'Nonsense. Nobody will mind. Deveron hospitality applies even at Tillicross and doesn't exclude rich Americans either. Now—to your right, these were the wine cellars, the kitchen and storage rooms. With some slight renovation they made a cosy flat for the Craigs while the restoration was in progress. These are the original vaulted ceilings, by the way—aren't they splendid?'

But my attention was nervously elsewhere. I was sure I had seen a dark shape, unmistakably female, disappear hastily along the corridor when Fraser ushered me in first.

Suddenly a door opened. 'Hello, Max,' said Fraser, quite unperturbed, to the man who emerged. 'Didn't realise you were at home.'

'Hi, Fraser. You're looking bright-eyed and bushy-tailed this morning, as they say in the best squirrel circles,' said Max grudgingly. 'If it's the folks you want at this godforsaken hour, they're away to Inverness. You sure don't look the way I feel.'

That was true. He looked, I thought, rather put out and embarrassed by this unexpected visit.

'Actually, it's the castle I want to show off today—

to this young lady.' Fraser introduced us, explaining my Deveron connection. 'A pity, if I'd known George was going to Inverness I'd have got him to check some fittings. Oh well, that's one of the disadvantages of being without a phone. I presume Pearl's with him?'

Max nodded and as the two men talked of various Tillicross matters, I observed that if there exists such a breed regarded by the Britisher as 'typical American' I was presently regarding this phenomenon. Max Craig, with his built-in accent, by the simple donning of a Stetson hat, could have graced any Western with his tall, rugged good looks. I could imagine him as a freckle-faced boy, then as the typical college boy, then the mature man. He was older than Fraser, nearer forty than thirty, but with an indefinable charm, an indestructible air of youth. Like so many attractive men, he would only improve with age. And I realised I knew another with the same inborn qualities: Ben Armstrong.

At that moment Fraser said: 'Max's ancestors, emigrated from nearby during the upheaval after the Highland clearances.'

'Yes indeed. That's why Uncle George and Aunt Pearl have always hankered to come back. They came one year on an ancestor-hunt, saw Tillicross and fell in love with it, met Fraser here in the local pub, and—bingo, you know the rest of the story.' He looked at his watch and frowned: 'I hate to rush you folks, but I have a lunch date over Elgin direction. However, we do have time for coffee. I'll make it while you show Miss Brent around.'

He indicated the room behind him. 'This here is the study-cum-spare bedroom, and my domain when I'm resident at Tillicross.' He led the way into two similar rooms, one obviously doing service as a guest bedroom. Then he touched a closed door: 'Kitchen here, Miss Brent, and begging your pardon and Fraser's, I guess I have to declare this room out of bounds.' He smiled apologetically. 'We all overslept this morning and I'm afraid the wee sma' hours aren't my favourite washing-up time, nor has my aunt a dish-washing machine. She says cheerfully there's no need when I come to stay—and I'd swear she saves them up for an entire month beforehand.'

He gave a comical sigh and added: 'Pearl would surely kill me for showing anyone, especially a lady, her kitchen with debris stacked high from last night's dinner.' While he was talking he had opened the study door and seized a large envelope which he handed to Fraser. 'We don't rise to a tourist guidebook yet, but these colour photos will give Miss Brent a fair idea of Tillicross before and after'—he looked at me— 'and the miracles Fraser Deveron has achieved. Yes, I mean it,' he said, as Fraser began denying such praise. 'Hey, Rusty, you want to come with me? Get some goodies?'

Rusty was disarmingly grateful and departed with alacrity, making me wonder as I followed Fraser up the spiral stair whether I had been wrong about her odd reactions in Deveron Castle last night. Was she just lazy when she got the chance?

Fraser stopped thumbing through the photographs: 'In the beginning—this was Tillicross when the Craigs bought it.'

Pre-restoration was a devastating sight, enough to daunt the most enthusiastic. Roofless stone walls stretched out pathetically into a grey winter sky. The north aspect also lacked a considerable part of one turret.

Fraser led me into a large room. 'This used to be the Great Hall—it looked like this.'

Only the carved stone fireplace and the windows in one wall were immediately recognisable from the photograph. Grass and weeds sprouted everywhere from roofless walls to stone flags, yet out of the hopeless debris quite incredibly had grown this magnificent room. Where once a small tree had made a determined bid for existence, now lay great skin rugs. A refectory table, Carolean chairs, old chests and an enormous library-bookcase added airs of authenticity and charm to the setting where solid walls, now weedless, were adorned by subdued tartan coverings, swords and claymores.

When I admired the latter Fraser looked pleased. 'Do you really like them? They came from Deveron and were my house-warming gift to the Craigs.'

I thought his idea charming and most thoughtful, for he had obviously taken great pains to know exactly what would most flatter Tillicross and please the owners. Up two wide steps was the room whose bow-fronted window looked down into the courtyard. 'This was once the solar, now it's the master bedroom.' There was a canopied bed, handsomely early Victorian furniture and an adjoining modern bathroom. When I exclaimed over its elegance and practicality, Fraser nodded approvingly :

'If we're to live in harmony with times past then there must be some compromise. Authenticity is one thing but I personally draw the line at a tin tub drawn up to the bedroom fire once a month—and such frequency was a matter to brag about in those days.'

We inspected two more rooms, functional but less impressive, and I asked : 'Have the Craigs any family?'

'Max is their only kin and more like a son than a nephew.'

'Do they have a housekeeper?'

'Alas no, Pearl deplores the fact that Tillicross is too remote for village help.'

'Is Max their only guest just now?'

He looked at me oddly. 'Yes.'

As we climbed another spiral I wondered who, then, was the girl I had glimpsed? And the room next to Max's downstairs had shown unmistakable evidence of female occupation, including a dark cape thrown over a chair and toilet articles spread on the dressing-table...

'There isn't much more,' said Fraser, opening the door with a flourish. 'Hey presto.'

A vast empty space yawned above us. Within a framework of rafters two additional floors were merely hinted at by the solid outlines of stone windows and fireplaces grotesquely situated at impossible levels above our heads. 'The Craigs decided they didn't need all those extra rooms.'

'It's simply gorgeous as it is, and I could move in tomorrow. Did you do it all yourself, Fraser?'

'Have a heart. I only superintended my designs and the actual building was carried out by a firm of contractors.'

'You are clever.'

He bowed. 'I'm glad you like it. Shows what could be done with Deveron, which isn't nearly as far gone as this, of course.' Half-way down the stairs, he stopped. 'Sorry—something I meant to check for Pearl when I was upstairs. You go down, I'll only be a moment.'

As I reached the ground-floor flat I heard voices and before I could decide whether it was the radio or not, the kitchen door opened stealthily and a girl disappeared into the room next to Max's study. But no mention was made of her presence, nor did she appear while we had coffee.

'Maybe you'd like a lift back to Deveron?' said Max. His offer was polite but rather reluctant, I felt, especially as his lunch date lay in the opposite direction. 'It would be no bother. Car's in the garage.' He nodded at Fraser. 'He decided that such amenities should be used and not seen in castles, so it's heavily disguised as the stables. No horses now, of course,' he added hastily, as if I might reasonably ask to inspect them.

Fraser pressed my arm warningly. 'Thanks but no. It's only two miles across country and I promised Candida I'd show her the countryside. She's a keen outdoor girl, you know.'

The 'Westerner' smiled, genuinely perplexed. 'You mean this lovely delicate creature actually *enjoys* walking on these non-existent tracks they call roads up here. Honey, they're only fit for horses and sheep—heaven knows what they *called* sheep-tracks in the old days.'

Fraser laughed. 'This one is actually an attractive sylvan path by the river. Come along, we mustn't delay Max any longer.' He picked up my suitcase and followed Max to the door.

'At least let me deliver that,' said Max, 'you can't walk back carrying luggage.'

'Luggage is too grand a word to describe it,' I said.

'It's only an overnight case, light as a feather,' said Fraser cheerfully.

As I listened to the two men exchanging farewell messages and various greetings to mutual acquaintances, the sun had reached the inside of the courtyard where it clung warmly to ancient walls, creating the promise and illusion of summer. I looked up at the lovely old house and thought: All is well within, for Tillicross had known gentle May mornings like this for more than four hundred years. Against such a measure of time, my small strife with Fraser and Morna's mysterious behaviour were transient as the life of that butterfly alighting on the wall beside me.

Perhaps Fraser read my thoughts, for he was watching me with the faintest of I-told-you-so glances.

Max held out a hand, regarded me with honest eyes and candid smile. 'Come again some day, Miss Brent,' he said softly. 'There'll always be a welcome awaiting you at Tillicross.'

I withdrew my hand hastily, my 'Thank you' cooler than his hospitality merited. I smiled at Fraser, indicating that I was ready to leave, for suddenly I wanted to be far away from Max's façade of charm and gallantry. Strange that although they would never meet, Ben and he would have been great chums, for they belonged to the same breed of men. In another ten years Ben would be exactly like Max Craig, his increasing years grown in attraction and personal magnitude, adding to inborn grace the poise of maturity. It didn't seem fair that fate should have led him to Deveron and that Fraser should be his only competition.

I made an unholy wish that Max could meet Ben's Debbie, and was rather short with Fraser when he said:

'Max is a great character, isn't he?'

I considered what I might have justly replied and remained silent instead with my thoughts, occasionally looking at Fraser with new-born respect and admiration for his work on Tillicross. And with another emotion, too—compassion.

Compassion, for I believed that I had uncovered one part of the mystery that intrigued me.

I wished I could be proved wrong, but there had been no mistaking the identity of the girl I had seen emerging from the kitchen when I went downstairs ahead of Fraser. And if her presence at Tillicross was entirely innocent, why then didn't she come forward and greet us, have coffee with us? And why was her name never mentioned at any time, even in the most casual way?

The evidence of my own eyes pointed in one undeniable direction. If Morna Keir was crippled, then Fraser was blind. Blind to the fact that Morna was blatantly deceiving him—with Max Craig.

10

As Fraser talked enthusiastically about castles and their problems quite oblivious to the one in his own life, to be faced sooner or later, I wanted suddenly to protect him from the kind of misery I was enduring over Ben. From the knife twist in the heart, where every day's awakening was to a sense of nightmare—then the realisation that it was no dream and this aching misery was reality to be lived through for yet another day.

There was nothing I could do to avert the coming disaster for Fraser, for like all who are deceived he would have to discover their treachery for himself. The farewell between the two men had indicated that Max was going back to the States soon. Perhaps the catastrophe could be delayed, or maybe Morna was only fascinated by the handsome Westerner old enough to be her father, while he was indulging his male vanity by flirting with a pretty young girl.

I sighed, hoping that Fraser would make a better recovery than I had done. After all, I had little to fill my life apart from the world of the Armstrongs and Perseus Plastics. The job with Rona, my home at Aynley House, all would come to an abrupt end once Ben married Debbie. My pride was too great to stay on as Rona's secretary and I could no longer regard myself as 'one of the family', as she implored me to do.

I wondered if there was a moral tale hidden in this morning at Tillicross and my discovery there, for my own life was in debris and I had to rebuild it as carefully as Fraser restored the castle. A new job, a place to live, some new roots—and perhaps in a far-off day too painful to consider just now, another love once Ben's image had faded from my heart.

I envied Fraser his dedicated life, for a man who could bring life again to the crumbling stones I had seen on the photographs was more than a genius. He was also something of a magician. I wished that the tissues of the human heart would mend as well, and that Fraser Deveron might wave a magic wand over my broken life and repair it as expertly as he had Tillicross Castle.

My thoughts had carried me quite unseeing and un-heeding at Fraser's side to a tiny track where he helped me over a stile.

'This leads through the foothills of Cairn Dever—we'll emerge in the castle grounds.'

A stream gurgled over rocks at our side and the twisting path was fringed with the yellow flame of gorse, while slender larches made a fragile arch over our heads. Here and there birds called to each other and near at hand a blackbird rent the air with its shrill warning cry.

'Oh, how beautiful it is.'

Fraser smiled approvingly. 'It's like this all the way —pleasanter than walking on roads, isn't it?'

I had thought the original road I travelled to Deveron unsurpassable in beauty, but walking on springy turf, with a stream, gentle sunshine and a new world putting on a show of passing splendour, as if for my special benefit, left me suddenly bereft of words. In this setting the superlatives seemed prosaic, inadequate. At my side, Fraser was silent and the quiet between us was like that of old friends whose understanding of the moment needs no words. Suddenly I knew for the first time what 'companionable silence' meant.

Fraser stopped, a warning hand on my arm. 'Don't speak,' he whispered. 'Look—over there.'

As an addition to this earthly paradise, a deer had come down to the river to drink. 'It's all right,' said Fraser, sniffing the air, 'we're on her windward side.' All frivolity over, the well-trained Rusty had dropped to the ground. She lay there watching intently, motionless, awaiting his further command.

The deer continued to drink delicately, quite unaware of us only a few yards away and, clinging closely to her side, a tiny fawn advanced cautiously and trotted on shaky legs to the water. Its tawny markings gave it a beauty not of this world and such perfection belonged to a world of fantasy, the fawn itself to Walt Disney's Bambi.

'A couple of days old,' whispered Fraser. 'They walk almost immediately.'

'Poor little thing . . .'

'It's nature's way of fitting the strongest to keep up with the herd as it moves. The weaklings, alas, are picked off by predators.'

Into this idyllic scene another deer advanced, then another.

'We seem to be getting the whole herd,' murmured Fraser. Although those beautiful haunted eyes from across the river darted at us—or seemed to—we were screened by trees. 'As long as we stay perfectly still, they'll not notice us.' I glanced down at Rusty, a dog carved from stone. Not even a whisker twitched.

Then came the final visitor. Beside him deer and their fawns dwarfed in size and magnificence. A stag with many-branched antlers proudly raised his head, sniffing the air.

Here was my Landseer painting, my 'Monarch of the Glen' come to superb life as he stood unmoving, outlined against the morning sky. It was too much.

'O World, I cannot hold thee close enough . . .' My eyes filled with sudden tears and, when I blinked them away, the skyline, the river bank, all were empty. It was as if the deer herd had never existed.

' "World, world, I cannot get thee close enough!
    Long have I known a glory in it all,
    But never I knew this . . ." '

I stopped embarrassed, and Fraser continued softly:

' "Here such a passion is
    As stretcheth me apart . . ." '

And, as if on cue, he turned and slowly took me in his arms. 'But at least I can hold thee close enough—for a little while.' He bent his head and kissed me very gently and with his lips touched the wet tears on my cheeks. 'You taste all salty.'

I must have looked surprised, for he said : 'Sorry, I shouldn't have done that, but it's your fault. You look extremely kissable.' He smiled and held me at arm's length. 'Now, what have I done? I've scared you again, you look as if you're about to retreat with the red deer. Stay a little while—I won't do it again, I promise.' He let go my hands and I stood watching him, suddenly conscious that my arms, so tightly clasped about his neck seconds ago, now hung limply at my side. He lifted my chin and held it. 'It wasn't intended as an insult, you know,' he said. 'Think of it as a compliment to the absent fiancé's taste.'

I shook my head. 'That wasn't the reason.'

But I couldn't explain. That I had never been kissed, except in an avuncular manner, by any man but Ben. And not for a long time there either. I couldn't tell Fraser that his kiss, chaste and seemly as it was, had made me realise what I had been missing. It awoke areas of sensuality which quite shocked me in their intensity. Far from flying indignantly away, I wanted to put my arms around him tightly and say : 'Kiss me again.' It was a revelation to realise that I must be sex-starved and how extraordinary to be overcome by such sensations, I thought, with a young man I hardly knew who didn't even greatly attract me, who, if anyone asked me, I would have readily dismissed as not my type.

I looked around me. This wild passionate country was the real culprit. It must be to blame, and the deer who had vanished entirely. They were obviously capable of anything, of awaking deep primitive instincts, or perhaps only making me see Candida Brent in a new light. Strange, for the first time I was glad to be young and free, even of Ben's domination, and the faint possibility that I might be desirable to other young men was quite delightful. That thought had not struck me before. Ben had never allowed me such illusions.

'Why so serious? Will he be angry?' asked Fraser.

'Who?'

'The absent fiancé. Isn't that what's worrying you? I'm not a bit sorry, really,' he added defiantly. 'But you can always blame me.'

I looked into his eyes. They were a curious blue that often goes with red hair and they were bright as polished stones. I wanted this moment to last. I wanted to stare into them for ever and never come back to the world which housed Ben and his kind, where cruelty and pain and defeat waited for me like an inescapable Greek chorus of misery, once I returned to York.

'Of course I'm not worried about Ben,' I said, and banished the mood by producing another absent love to break up this idyll so unexpected, this wild dream growing somewhere deep in my heart.

'Of course I'm not worried,' I repeated. 'Will Morna be angry too?' I asked flippantly.

'Morna? Good heavens no—she'll just laugh.'

If my suspicions about Max Craig were correct, then she had good reason to 'just laugh'. I let go of his hand and began to walk ahead along the track. I was glad it was straight and narrow at this junction, the Biblical allegory seemed rather well timed. Deliberately I turned my back on the magic that had so lightly brushed us—and so briefly too. A magic that still lurked everywhere, filling my blood with wanton dreams of heather that might be a warm seductive bed made specially for lovers, the warm sun above our heads, a blanket of desire.

'Tell me about Ben,' said Fraser, making conversation.

Briskly I walked, snatching up a long strand of grass and shredding it carefully. 'Ben. There's nothing much to tell.'

Behind me there was a moment's silence while Fraser digested this information. 'Then tell me about this secret room in the castle. What was it like?'

I described it exactly. The cobwebbed bed, the narrow window, the sparse furnishing. 'But you must know about it. Otherwise, how did the oil-painting of Morna get there?'

The path had widened and we were walking side-by-side again.

'Morna?' he asked. 'How come?'

'Morna as the White Rose,' I explained patiently.

We had our first glimpse of the castle as we turned the corner. It stood grey and grim, a huge fortress pillowed in trees.

'Describe this picture,' said Fraser.

'Well, it's life-size. Of Morna in a hooded cape, holding a white rose in her hand.'

'A white rose in her hand,' repeated Fraser excitedly. 'Candida—describe it again, every detail you can remember.'

I described it exactly, cracks and all, how I thought the damp had probably got at it, and, knowing little about painting, that had made it look like a genuine antique. 'You should really persevere with that accidental technique,' I concluded. 'You might make a fortune with it in picture-faking, if it stands up to a good light. The light, of course, was terrible in that room. It's probably not nearly so convincing by daylight.'

Fraser ignored my comments and I began to wonder from his serious face if I had insulted his attempts at painting portraits. He looked at me sharply and asked: 'Did your great-uncle ever mention a painting like this to you?'

Below us lay Fraser's kingdom, the caravan like a child's bright toy, Jeannie Deveron's cottage in the lane. Beside it the Murder Field, looking like a large untidy heap of stones and heather. Beyond the village, the main road. But in the foreground dominating all else was Deveron Castle.

Fraser took my hand. 'My dear Candida, I think I owe you an apology for doubting your word.'

'So you believe me now. What convinced you?'

'Something you didn't know about.'

'What was that?'

'Are you quite, quite sure old Jamie never mentioned a painting of the White Rose of Deveron?'

'Absolutely sure.'

Fraser was silent for a moment, then said, almost to himself, 'Chances were he'd never heard of it. That piece of scandal was kept very quiet within the family.'

'Fraser, I haven't a clue what you're talking about. How could Great-Uncle Jamie have mentioned the painting? Morna must have been about twelve then and your painting is of a woman—and a fairly recent likeness.'

He shook his head. 'It's not my painting, Candida. I've never painted Morna in my life. For one thing, I'm a good draughtsman maybe, but I'm hopeless when it comes to drawing people, let alone painting them life-size in oils. As for that antiquing process, as you call it . . .' He smiled. 'You do me too much credit—if I could do that I certainly would be forging old masters and selling them to millionaires to get a roof on Deveron again.'

119

He paused. 'The really interesting part of all this is that I had no idea until now that Morna resembled, even remotely, Margaret the White Rose of Deveron.'

'Well, I have to be honest. These were all first impressions. Even in the poor light I wouldn't be prepared to swear that her hair colour is exact, nor perhaps the colour of her eys. But the overall resemblance. *That* is quite staggering.'

'It happens occasionally. The family throwback, I mean.' Suddenly he gripped my arm. 'Candida— I'm almost certain what you have discovered is the Allan Ramsay portrait.'

Allan Ramsay. The name meant nothing to me.

'You haven't heard of him? Oh, well, that's scarcely surprising, really, for an English girl. Allan Ramsay was an eighteenth-century Scottish portrait painter of some renown.' He paused. 'Remember I told you that the castle door was never locked and the only burglary we ever had was at the turn of the century?'

'I remember.'

'What I didn't tell you was that the only thing stolen was a portrait. Allan Ramsay's "White Rose".'

II

Fraser's excitement over the stolen portrait was irresistible.

'I expect it was very valuable, considering the prices paintings are sold for these days.'

Fraser shook his head. 'When it was stolen there wasn't quite the same boom in antiques, and an Allan Ramsay wouldn't have fetched the astronomic prices we are accustomed to these days. There were some pieces in the house much more portable, easier to lift and much more valuable at that time. I can hardly believe it—Candida, do you realise that if this *is* Allan Ramsay's "White Rose of Deveron", with its romantic history, all my troubles over restoring Deveron could quite possibly be at an end.'

'What would it fetch in auction?'

The figure he suggested made me blink, and even Ben would have been impressed. Deep in thought, he skirted the caravan and hurried towards the castle. I followed him up the spiral staircase and he walked quickly into the Great Hall, where he paused and said :

'Do you think you could possibly find this room again?'

'Of course, it was very gloomy outside and I was rather confused with the directions, but I think I could find it,' I said confidently. 'We went to the left here and it was half-way along one of the corridors, in the wall panelling. It must have been marked on the outside to indicate it was a door, but it was too dark for me to see it clearly.'

'What are we waiting for? Let's go.'

A careful but futile inspection of every piece of panelling on that corridor led us into a similar activity in the next—and the next. We gave up and branched to the left, very hopefully but without success. Another corridor and another, each a replica of the one we had left, and each linked to the floors above and below by a fragment of identical spiral staircase.

Finally, almost in tears, I had to admit defeat.

Fraser sighed. 'Certainly none of the panels have visible handles. Was there nothing, no distinguishing mark you can remember on any of them? Think hard.'

'Oh, Fraser, I just can't remember,' I wailed. 'You can see for yourself how difficult it is. Even in this light the panelling is dark and shadowed, can you imagine what it was like late at night? I just can't remember any identification marks—honestly.'

All I could remember was how cold it had been, how cold I was and afraid and confused. The confusion of nightmare, I thought, uneasily. Could that have been the answer? Had Fraser's earlier tour and the warning that the corridors were in a maze pattern have struck some deep-seated childhood terror after being lost in the maze in our local park, followed by a fear of being lost in the dark? Then had sleeping in a strange and ancient bed made me dream the rest?

'Don't worry,' said Fraser. 'I'm not blaming you,' he added with a forced smile. 'Now, what about this panel in the room that turned out to be a corner cupboard?'

'It came out on a ruined spiral stair, but as I had run down ten, maybe twenty, stairs, I didn't count them—when I climbed it again I couldn't even be sure that where it emerged into the corridor was on the same floor as the secret room.'

'A ruined stair. Let me see, there are two. On the north and east side.'

'I could see Cairn Dever—or part of it, I think—through the narrow window.'

'Perhaps we're getting somewhere at last. Come along, we'll try the north side first.'

Down two corridors and on to a stair with panelling to the left-hand, just as it had been when I emerged. For a while, as Fraser systematically tapped the panelling and all sounded hollow, I was hopeful.

'I doubt it,' he said, shaking his head. 'Let's try the east.' Here again was a gleam of hope, there were noises and signs of a rookery. After a while Fraser too was beaten. 'There's absolutely no indication of any door in these panels,' he said with a sigh, sitting down on the stairs beside me wearily.

'Haven't you got any original plans of the castle?'

'They were lost long ago, alas. Or perhaps Alexander Deveron intended that they should be, so that he could keep his little secrets.' He stood up and took my hands. 'We'll have to give up, I'm afraid. We would need to tackle all the panelling with a crowbar to find anything here,' he added with an exasperated sigh.

Gloomily we walked across the Great Hall, then suddenly Fraser stopped. 'There's one avenue as yet unexplored. The old library. My father had a mania for collecting press cuttings—anything about Deveron or his friends hereabouts. While he was still reasonably fit, he had a dream of writing a family history.'

'Perhaps there's something about the burglary.'

The library, with its magnificent double doors, had a musty smell of old leather-bound volumes long unopened. Birds had come down the chimney. Their droppings and feathers were everywhere and some small corpses too of those who had dashed themselves to death trying to escape from their prison. There was even evidence of nesting operations.

'Fortunately most of the more valuable books are behind glass doors,' said Fraser, eyeing the melancholy scene. 'This was my father's favourite room, he spent hours alone, researching and reading. My earliest memories are of being with him at this desk,' he added, blowing the thick dust off its top. 'When Mother left him he used to sit here for hours—in that chair. It was his favourite.'

I looked at the tall old-fashioned leather chair, with its indentations on back and seat, where he had rested his head, and the arms scuffed and darkened by his hands resting there, brooding away the lonely hours. It made me feel sad and uncomfortable, as if, could I but narrow my eyes, I might still see the shade of the sad old man regretting the work he had never finished.

Fraser had opened a cupboard in the desk and taken out a large box file. 'Here it is, just as I remember it,' he said, triumphantly blowing away the dust. 'Father was very methodical, all these cuttings should be in chronological order.' He thumbed through the yellowed papers. 'Got it. This is what I'm after. The press report of the burglary. "Burglary at Deveron Castle",' he read: ' "During the absence of Lady Hilda Deveron in London last week, the castle was the scene of a daring robbery. Owing to the presence of mind and courage of the estate factor, who saw a light in the direction of the Great Hall and went to investigate, the thieves were disturbed and got away with only one portrait, the Allan Ramsay 'White Rose of Deveron'. Mr. Andrew Keir, the factor, when interviewed by our news reporter said : 'As you know, the laird of Deveron is an invalid and when I saw a moving light I decided to take a look.' Thanks to his presence of mind many other valuable and irreplaceable items smaller than the portrait were untouched . . ." ' Fraser paused and added dryly : 'What an irresistible invitation to future burglars ! I wonder they didn't take it up.'

I thought for a moment. 'Why should a thief steal it and then hide it in a secret room ? Did he perhaps mean to come back for it ?'

'If he did, then that presupposes something very important.'

'You mean that he was familiar with the geography of the castle.'

'Yes. Think about it. Why should a thief steal only a painting that would have taken two men to carry it out—and a considerable effort to conceal it inside—remember they didn't have much in the way of fast cars or vans in those days. Where were they intending to take it—or to dispose of it? A life-size family portrait is fairly un-negotiable, and untransportable—unless it is removed from its frame.'

'The painting I saw, if it's the same one was in a heavy gold frame.'

'Mm. That doesn't surprise me, in fact it rather confirms my own idea about this robbery. Let's think back. This was during Grandmamma's fairly frequent sojourns in London, where she was supposedly leading a life of great wickedness to say nothing of paralysing extravagance. My father often hinted that rumour had it that she was not unconnected with its disappearance, as she had been systematically stripping Deveron Castle of its valuable contents so she could keep up with Bertie's royal set. And since the laird was in a wheelchair, I don't suppose he could do much to stop her trips to London and the frequent visits of Bertie and his entourage for the shooting at Deveron.'

'But if she stole it for gain, why then didn't she dispose of it? Surely she had plenty of contacts in London to smuggle it out of the country?'

'Let's go back to the beginning. You asked why should a burglar steal it and conceal it in the castle. Perhaps he was disturbed and meant to come back for it.' He paused. 'But surely you have by now guessed the thief's identity? No? The answer, my dear Candida, is simple. There was no thief, no burglary. It's as plain as the nose on your face. Grandfather arranged the break-in when she was safely out of the way, to save the most treasured possession—not the most valuable by any means—but the one dearest to the family, from his wife's greed. Deveron meant nothing to her, except as a setting for her social life in Scotland.'

'So that's why he had it hidden in a secret room, probably with the help of some loyal servant, if he was himself quite incapable of moving it.'

'Exactly. There were no hints of a priest-hole in early records of the house, but obviously Grandfather expected his rapacious wife to outlive him and inherit Deveron, so if he discovered anything, he wasn't going to let her know.'

He paused. 'There is another possibility, of course. That the whole deal was instigated by some loyal servant or servants who knew where the secret room lay. Remember servants in those days often lived their whole lives in the castle. Maybe someone devoted to the old man had a bright idea of saving the portrait.'

'You mean Andrew Keir?'

'Who better? Incidentally, he was Morna's great-grandfather. However, it doesn't help us much,' he added gloomily, 'a probable guess at the thief's identity, but no way of finding out how—or more particular where—he disposed of the portrait.'

He was putting the papers into the file again, turning them over, when he picked up a small yellowed fragment of newspaper. 'Hello, what's this? It must have escaped the paper clip. Good heavens, listen to this. "Tragic death of Deveron factor. Andrew Keir died of a heart attack last night, four days after he courageously scared off burglars in Deveron Castle"—

and so on. It ends: "The laird said Keir had been in very poor health lately." ' Fraser put down the scrap of paper. 'And moving that great picture single-handed wouldn't help him much either. I guess his unfortunate demise was brought about by negotiating the portrait about these corridors.'

'Why don't you ask Morna? It's just possible she may know something.'

Fraser shook his head. 'I doubt it. The family went down to England in that generation and only returned a few years ago when Morna's father retired early, as I told you.' He gave me a speculative look. 'Talking of Morna, you say she was exactly like the girl in the portrait—and the one who led you to this vanishing room.'

'Oh yes. And then when I did get back to the master bedroom I had this awful dream. Of Morna, or the White Rose—but it was me in the dream, racing up Cairn Dever away from the Redcoat soldiers. She was wounded, they shot her . . .' and I closed my eyes blotting out the next few minutes of that nightmare of horror. 'And finally they killed her with their bayonets.'

'Very finally, if the legend is anything to go by,' said Fraser grimly.

'It was by the shrine and she was praying. I think she was already dead before—the rest—happened.'

'Before God, I hope so. I hate to think of any girl suffering a death ignoble as that one.'

'It was all terribly vivid. You have no idea—it was quite sickeningly real. I can't explain. Like a waking dream. As if it was all actually happening—and to me—at that moment.'

'Like your adventure with Morna and the secret room, you mean,' he asked idly.

'Exactly. As a matter of fact there was precious little difference between either.'

He was silent and, looking at him, I realised I had fallen into the trap laid by his casual question. With a few words I had only to look into his face to know I had undone all his conviction, undermined all his newly built confidence in my story.

He gave an exasperated sigh. 'Come along, we might as well go back to the caravan and have something to eat. I'm starving.' As we walked downstairs he said: 'Perhaps it was just a dream, Candida. Apparently you do dream very vividly. If there isn't any secret room, then there isn't any other plausible explanation. Maybe you've even had a conversation with the old man about the portrait of the White Rose and you've forgotten it, but the associations of sleeping in the castle aroused it again from your subconscious.'

'Then how did I know about the broken spiral?'

'Well—I did take you on a tour of the corridors and warn you about the maze pattern. In your excitable state such dreams were easy . . .'

And instead of feeling indignant about his doubting my word, I realised he was only putting into words the qualms I had already experienced.

He took my arm gently. 'It doesn't matter, Candida. Honestly—come along. Cheer up.'

I had to be satisfied with this explanation, but I didn't like it. Surely I could still differentiate between dreams and reality, even vivid dreams? Had Great-Uncle Jamie mentioned a missing portrait that I had forgotten until I came to Deveron? The old man had talked so much, it was difficult to recall many of the things he had told us—fact or fiction.

Of course, there was another explanation, so monstrous that I refused even to contemplate it. And I certainly wasn't inclined to mention this theory to Fraser.

Out in the open again, Rusty nuzzled my hand, begging for a good romp. 'I wish you could talk, old girl. You saw it all, didn't you?'

'A pity she didn't go with you, because she could have led us right to the spot. She's a trained gun-dog —in fact, I'm surprised and annoyed that she disobeyed my command. She was to stay with you, for I thought you might wander out and get lost—or frightened. I wonder why she refused to go?'

'I think she was scared of the dark,' I said in her defence, remembering her abject misery, her implorings that I should remain with her.

'Oh, what nonsense. You obviously weren't firm enough and she was being lazy. She just wanted to snooze by the fire. You saw the way she behaved at Tillicross when she got the chance.'

It could be true. But then there was that other explanation, simple but terrible. Oh, Fraser, I thought, why can't you have a *guess* at why she didn't follow me, when all the other explanations have proved wrong? I said: 'You must have been very late leaving last night.'

He frowned. 'About three, I think.'

'Did you go back with Morna?' I asked innocently.

He gave me a hard look. 'Of course not. She didn't have her car. Max met us at the garage and drove us to Tillicross, then back to Deveron. After all, Morna's a working girl, you know. Has to be up to make her father's breakfast and get things moving at the garage by eight-thirty. Why all the questions?' he added gently.

'I couldn't sleep after my vivid dream about the White Rose, so I got out of bed, went to the bathroom and when I came back I saw you coming up the lane. It was five by my watch. And you were carrying a spade over your shoulder.'

'Me? Carrying a spade over my shoulder?' He laughed out loud. 'How incredible. My dear Candida, don't you think you were dreaming again?'

And the whole day was ruined for me. Our precious morning, with so much shared. Those cherished moments by the river when the red deer came down to drink. An idyll, like a crystal ball, shattered, ruined.

I was angry again. Furiously so. For this time I knew without doubt that he lied.

But why? Why?

And when we reached the caravan the police car was already waiting.

12

'Miss Brent.'

And there were the two policemen from Act 1 of my Drama at Deveron, the police station at Muldoune Bridge. 'This is your wallet? Would you please examine the contents?'

The owners of the mill had returned earlier than expected that afternoon and handed it over to the police, who had gone to a lot of trouble on my behalf, knowing that I was stranded.

I was most grateful. I signed the receipt and there were mutual good wishes as the car sped away. I watched them disappear, thinking how strange the measure of time, two days that seemed like two decades, since the curtain was raised on my misfortunes at Muldoune Bridge. I looked across at Fraser, who had now taken on the role—almost—of old and trusted friend in so short a time, and thought how, had I not lost my wallet, we would never have met, I would never have seen Deveron either.

He said : 'Well, you're free to go now—at last.' I wondered if I detected a tone of regret, a wistful look in his eye, but the next moment he was consulting his watch in practical manner. 'I'm afraid you'll be too late for the train tonight. Like to stay until tomorrow?'

'Oh, yes, please,' I said, hoping I didn't sound ridiculously eager.

The rain, which had been restraining itself with difficulty, began with renewed frenzy and I was glad of the hitherto unsuspected snugness of the caravan. We prepared a quite unspectacular meal of chicken and salad which somehow acquired festive proportions. Or was that illusion the effect of the wine Fraser produced? Festivity tinged with regret, the parting of old friends, for this was undoubtedly our farewell meal. There was no longer an excuse for my staying at Deveron.

'We must keep in touch,' said Fraser, rather lamely.

'Yes, I'll send you a Christmas card.' Disappointment was considerable, it was also out of the question when I had led him to believe I was going home to the man I loved and would shortly marry, the man whose ring I still wore. And hadn't he already clearly indicated his devotion to Morna?

The momentary awkwardness passed and our conversation drifted back to the fascinating topic of the missing Allan Ramsay portrait and the secret room. My flagging confidence bolstered by food and wine, I said: 'Let's have another look. It must be there somewhere.'

'All right,' said Fraser. 'There's a lull in the storm —a good omen, surely.'

'Of course it is. I'm sure we'll find it this time. There must be something to identify it that's escaped my notice.'

But as we roamed the castle's gloomy corridors I stayed as close to Fraser and Rusty as I dared. The maze of ill-lit panelled corridors was hardly an entertaining prospect on a dark and gloomy day, with the rain pouring down the windows with renewed fervour, adding to the general sense of melancholy desolation.

Once again, wearily I had to admit defeat. Looking at Fraser, trying to explain how baffled I was, I felt he was quieter more withdrawn than ever, disappointment mingled with actual distrust this time. He no longer needed to say the words that hung in the air : 'You dreamed it all. It's a figment of your imagination.'

As strangers who had been momentarily close we had now reverted to the wilderness of unknowing again. Acutely sensitive to atmosphere, I suspected a barrier of reserve, of new shyness, had grown between us. And I sensed relief in his announcement that he had to go to Muldoune Bridge to meet a friend from student days, breaking his journey there on a business trip to the north of Scotland. He would borrow one of the hiring cars from Keirs' garage.

'Sorry I have to go and leave you on your last evening. Will you manage on your own?'

'Of course. I have plenty to read,' I said brightly.

Fraser pondered for a moment. 'Look, perhaps you'd be happier sleeping here in the caravan tonight. Sleeping in the castle never bothers me.'

I was easily persuaded and before he left he showed me how to let down the bed without snapping off my wrists, how to make tables spring back into walls, so I had plenty of mechanical troubles to occupy my mind for the first half-hour after his departure. When I considered it at all, I felt that our parting was accomplished with mutual relief.

Later I settled down, determined to read, but the paperback thriller I had chosen as companion for the long evening ahead seemed tame stuff compared with my present circumstances. I found my eyes were scanning the pages without the words registering as my thoughts constantly drifted to the unresolved mystery at Deveron. Putting aside the book with an exasperated sigh, I tried the radio, but the competition of heavy rain at such close quarters made listening to music an impossibility.

A tap at the door and I opened it to Jeannie Deveron.

She peered past me into the caravan. 'Mr. Fraser? Is he here?'

I said he had left an hour ago and thought privately it was rather surprising that she hadn't seen him go past her cottage, when normally she missed so little.

'He didn't leave any instructions about preparing the bedroom at the castle again. And I wondered, seeing that you were staying another night presumably, whether you would like me to light the fire?'

'I'm sleeping in the caravan here, but Mr. Fraser will be staying in the castle.'

She gave me a hard look. 'I hope everything was to your satisfaction, Miss Brent,' she said stiffly. 'I tried to make you as comfortable as I could, you know. It was very short notice and the room hadn't been slept in for some considerable time . . .'

'Oh, of course. It was splendid. But actually I didn't sleep very well. My own fault,' I added hastily. 'You see, I'm not used to sleeping in such a vast area on my own . . .'

'Most folks are nervous when they sleep in the castle for the first time. It's a very old bed, you see,' she said heavily. 'Generations have been born and died in it and suchlike things cling. Folk who are sensitive can feel them.' She paused. 'Then there are the other things, too, that go on all the time.'

I was conscious of my heart hammering at my ribs. 'What other things?'

She looked beyond me down the road, as if she could see it all. 'Oh, things like the Murder Field down there, that happened so long ago. The past isn't gone, Miss Brent, it's still with us, walking hand-in-hand with the present. Sometimes if we have the sight we can see and feel it all happening at this very moment.'

I took a deep breath. This was exactly my own re-action when the White Rose or whoever she was had led me along the corridors at Deveron Castle last night. 'Are you trying to tell me that the castle has a ghost, Mrs. Deveron?' I asked, with a poor imitation of a disbelieving smile.

She shook her head. 'I'm not *trying* to tell you any-thing you don't know already, Miss Brent.' She nod-ded sharply. 'I think you know very well what I'm talking about—you feel things too, don't you?'

It was an opportunity to find out for certain—and I snatched at it. 'Have you ever seen anything strange in the castle?'

She sighed. 'No, never. Not in there. But you have, haven't you?'

In the silence that followed she stared hard at me, fixing me with her eyes, almost willing me to tell her all that had happened. I turned away quickly, breaking our shared moment.

'I had better get on with my work.' On the step she paused. 'I saw the police car going down the lane earlier. Nothing serious, I hope, for Mr. Fraser?'

'Actually they came to see me.'

'You?' And she looked startled, frightened now. 'What did they want with you?' she demanded. 'Was it to do with the old man?'

At first I didn't know what she was talking about, then I remembered her earlier fever of curiosity when she thought I had come to Deveron to search for my great-uncle, the old shepherd who had vanished and whose body had not yet been recovered. Suddenly I was acutely aware that this was the real purpose of her visit.

'Have they heard something about him?'

'Not that I know of. The police car was merely returning the wallet to me.'

'Wallet? Which wallet—whose was that? Where did they find it?' All these questions were directed at me in a nervous staccato manner.

'It was mine, Mrs. Deveron.' And she gave an audible sigh of relief. 'I left it in the woollen mill at Muldoune Bridge. Remember I told you when I couldn't pay you for my bed and-breakfast yesterday?'

'Oh that,' she said scornfully. 'I had forgotten.'

What a state she is in, I thought, almost as if she had

135

stolen it herself. 'Well, I must away now.'

An idea came to me. 'Mrs. Deveron, you've lived here a long time.'

'All my life, off and on.'

'Did—has anyone ever mentioned the possibility of a secret room in the castle? I mean, one only known to a few people in the family—a room that isn't on any plans or even visible from the outside. A sort of priest-hole?'

She thought about it. 'There are always rumours like that, but most of them are fairy-tales. Big castles have reputations for secret rooms, there's famous ones like Glamis Castle.' She shook her head. 'But I've never heard anything of the sort about Deveron, and I've been in and out doing things for the family, cleaning and so forth and helping at table in the laird's day. Aye, and look after young Mr. Fraser since his father died. I would swear I know every inch of the place.'

Now for the first time I really doubted the evidence of my own eyes—or my own dreams. Surely if Jeannie Deveron who knew everything about the glen and the castle—and the inhabitants of both—said there was no secret room, the odds seemed overwhelmingly large in the direction of my over-fertile imagination.

After she departed I took up my book again. It was eight o'clock, too early to go to bed, I thought regretfully, with the long evening stretched out in front of me. Full of melancholy, I stared out of the window at the lovely panorama of the Glen of Deveron, with its hint of the tender yellows, the subtle greens of early-summer. The next instant, triumphant through the heavy cloud, rose a blue float of sky, the sombre greyness dissolved and the sun shone.

I knew now what I would do. I would go for a walk. Outside I hesitated, then decided to explore the other side of the castle, see if I could identify the fir-clad slope I had glimpsed from the narrow slit of window high above my head in the secret room. This identification was easier imagined than accomplished, for not only was Deveron Castle surrounded on three sides by fir-clad slopes, but the ground underfoot was extremely wet and treacherous. In no time at all I was drenched. My shoes offered no resistance to the soaked undergrowth of weeds and long grass while raindrops descended from the heavy trees in avalanches and found a resting-place down the back of my neck.

When I encountered the greenish statues in their little glade it gave me quite a turn. A good soaking had not improved their moth-eaten condition, so that they now looked like drowned creatures, ghastly and sinister in the dim light. My further adventurings were forestalled by a drift of stream, a large nettle bed and much overgrown shrubbery locked in a fierce battle for supremacy.

Uncomfortable, miserable and thoroughly disgruntled, I retreated again to the caravan, where I changed my shoes, shook out my raincoat and went down to the village. I had an urgent desire to hear another human voice and a sudden attack of homesickness for those I loved. I decided I would phone Rona and ask her to send someone to meet my train at York. Aynley House involved two rather long and tedious bus journeys and I hated the thought of arriving unannounced and finding myself in the midst of some family celebration involving Ben's new fiancée, where my unexpected appearance would smite the entire Armstrong clan like some latter-day ghost of Banquo. I could take a taxi at a cost of several pounds, an expense which Ben would not have given a second thought, but such high living made me wince.

I had reached Jeannie's cottage when I realised the threatening sky wasn't joking. Seconds later it erupted in heavy spots of rain. I decided that as Mrs. Deveron was probably still absorbed by domestic duties in the castle—for the cottage looked very still and empty—I would ignore the family curse by sneaking swiftly across the Murder Field, risking blasphemy, sacrilege and the rest. Perhaps I might beat the approaching storm, which would otherwise catch me before I had time to trot around two sides of the triangle.

I hesitated for only a moment. After all, I wasn't particularly superstitious—I would take refuge in being only half-Deveron and, frankly, I felt pretty cursed as it was. Having lost my *raison d'être* when Ben Armstrong walked out of my life, I didn't feel much else could happen to worsen my present situation.

Half-way across, stumbling over roots, blundering through heather, I changed my mind about this being the quick way to civilisation. My progress was exhaustingly slow, hurrying was impossible, steady walking extremely difficult. Angrily I began to consider the speed I would have made keeping to the main road. By the time I had twice ricked my ankles on concealed roots, I began to realise more than superstition kept the Deveron folk from using Murder Field as a shortcut to the village.

At that moment, as if to take a mean advantage of my predicament, the storm burst over my head. I took to my heels, which was most unwise, as I shot forward full length and, trying to save myself from further disaster, gave my wrist a nasty wrench.

Rubbing bruised knees and examining other injuries, I noticed I had escaped a worse encounter from a broken bottle which lay mere inches away. Someone

138

wasn't perturbed by the Deveron curse, for the bottle was new, the label still attached proudly advertised the well-known brand of malt whisky from the distillery where Great-Uncle Jamie had once worked as night-watchman.

Near where I knelt among the heather, nursing my wounds, was an overhang of grass and boulder, but, as I looked closer, I saw something that aroused my curiosity. The overhang concealed a small crude wooden door.

I gave it an experimental push. Doors in Deveron seemed to specialise in that quality of being without visible means of opening—or locking apparently. It didn't move, so I gave it a hearty shove. This was accompanied by a splintering noise and I found my-self shooting forward as the door flattened before me. A moment later I was like Alice in Wonderland, with my top half fast vanishing down a small tunnel.

In the thirty seconds I lay there any number of romantic notions flashed through my head. I didn't even have the wit to be afraid. My first contemplation was the existence of treasure trove, the end to Fraser Deveron's misfortunes and a new deal for the glen. Had I stumbled on the true reason for keeping all those curious eyes out of the Murder Field?

Then I noticed the smell. Sweet but highly unpleas-ant, distinctly decomposition, like a very old vegetable patch with nastier overtones. My second notion— hadn't Jeannie Deveron told me this was once a Pictish burial—had I stumbled on archaeological treasure—an earth house, a Beaker burial?

Now that my eyes were getting accustomed to the gloom, I noticed a shape. I put out an experimental hand, touched a bundle of rags, then something hard —like leather.

Struggling backwards into the daylight and with much more courage that I realised I possessed, I grovelled in my handbag until I came to book-matches of Perseus Plastic, carried at Ben's instigation as advertising for the firm, rather than any previous necessity of mine. I struck one. In the damp it fizzled out. Leaning inside, I struck another with more success. The little flare lit up the scene in its entirety, for there wasn't much room to spare.

A man sat in front of me, huddled in the attitude of one who sleeps. It took only a second to realise that this sleep was eternal. He was very dead and had been so for a long time. Fortunately his head was averted, so I was spared the more grisly details.

He was still a big man, even allowing for the shrinkage of death. He was old, too, with an unforget-table thatch of white hair and beard.

And so I know whom I had found. Great-Uncle Jamie Faser Deveron, missing shepherd. And judging by the evidence of dusty whisky bottles all around him, pickled nicely in alcohol, just the way he would have chosen to go.

13

I had to tell someone.

I had no suspicion of murder. My stupefied mind registered only a dead man. A dead man who for some extraordinary reason got his kicks out of drinking whisky in a tiny dug-out in the middle of the scene of a sixteenth-century Deveron massacre.

I realised the urgency of telling someone quickly. Jeannie—or Fraser. Or going to the village and raising the alarm? Yes, that would be best. But as I stood up I saw an impressive black Rolls cruising along the lane in the direction of the castle.

Fraser had returned in style. I stumbled back across the Murder Field, opened the cottage door, bawled for Jeannie, just in case. There was no reply, so I hurried on towards the castle.

I had almost reached it when I was conscious of eyes watching me from above. And there she was. Mrs. Deveron regarding me most intently from what was undoubtedly the window of the master bedroom. I noted her stillness, her agonised expression. It was as if all distance between us was diminished and her terror and anguish communicated itself by some strange telepathy between us. Sickened, I stopped in my tracks, knowing without any words that she had watched the whole episode on the Murder Field, which she would see clearly from her vantage point. I also knew instinctively that in some way she was implicated and had always known that the old man was dead in Murder Field.

Even as I dropped the hand I had raised in greeting, she stepped hastily back, pretending she hadn't seen me. I felt the cold shiver of disaster slide across my shoulders as I ran towards the castle door.

Thank goodness Fraser had already arrived and I wouldn't be alone when I told my story. I found myself remembering so many small but highly significant things about previous encounters with Jeannie Deveron. Her guilty behaviour whenever I mentioned my great-uncle, her terror that I should go across the

Murder Field. I was greatly relieved to know there was now some probable explanation for the noise I had heard when I had slept at the cottage. The sounds of battle—and I remembered how insistent she had been that I did hear them, yet Fraser, living here all his life, confessed that he had never heard anything of the sort.

A sound training in crime from reading thrillers as my favourite form of relaxation made me suspect she might have stage-managed this noisy event to scare me off, perhaps with the aid of a tape recording turned up loud. I remembered among the otherwise simple furnishings, a handsome radiogram, which she said belonged to her absent son Joe.

Joe. Hadn't Fraser told me that my great-uncle constantly quarrelled with the Deverons when he was drunk, and tried forcibly to evict them from what he still believed was rightfully his cottage? Fraser had said that Joe was an ugly customer.

I felt certain I had stumbled on to the truth. It explained Joe's disappearance from the glen, his mother's terror. Perhaps on one of these encounters with the old shepherd there had been a fight, Jamie had been killed and they had hidden him in the Murder Field.

Poor Jeannie, I thought with compassion for her misguidance. I hoped she wasn't to be any further implicated. The doting mother of a ne'er-do-well son, I suspected she was more sinned against than sinning.

The car parked near the door was a distinct improvement as hired cars went. How fortunate that Fraser was on such excellent terms with the Keirs' garage. He had informed me earlier that there were only two cars for hiring: the Volkswagen and a larger car kept for special occasions, such as VIP visits, weddings and funerals.

I ran up the spiral stair, expecting to find Fraser and Rusty with Jeannie in the master bedroom. I flung open the door, ready to confront them with my revelations. Only there was nobody there. The room was silent, empty except for the fire Jeannie had lit, sluggishly crackling away behind a fireguard. I looked into the bathroom, then ran into the corridor, listening hopefully for some distant sound of voices.

There were none.

'Fraser—Mrs. Deveron—are you there?'

And a small scuffle made my scalp crawl. For although nobody responded to my call, the sound I heard was undoubtedly that of footsteps, slipping along stealthily in my direction. Somewhere very close at hand.

'Mrs. Deveron, is that you?' I shouted firmly. And the small scuffling stopped suddenly, as if the listener had sinister reasons for staying unidentified.

'Fraser, Fraser,' I called boldly. At least my voice sounded reassuringly normal and unafraid. 'Fraser.'

From far away a voice answered: 'Candida—is that you?'

It came from the other side of the Great Hall and doubtless because there were strange echoes, it didn't sound at all like Fraser's voice. In fact, it sounded like —someone else . . .

Oh damn, I thought furiously, near to tears, there I go again with my hallucinations.

'Fraser—I'm in the bedroom. Please come—I have something to show you.'

The scuffle of footsteps was agitated now, loud enough to be angry and male. Only instead of coming to me, they retreated, grew steadily fainter.

'Fraser—Fraser,' I shouted. Then I listened. Nothing—but yes, there behind me, the scuffle of faint steps. This time there was no mistaking them. Now they were light and quick, a woman's stealthy foot-steps.

'Mrs. Deveron, are you there?'

Again silence, followed by a small movement as if someone trying to walk quietly on tiptoe, struck a creaking board. It was when I thought I also detected heavy breathing close at hand that I panicked and took to my heels, calling 'Fraser!' and running in the direction where I had imagined I heard that other voice.

My action was instinctive and it was also the very worst move I could have made. Two minutes later I was rushing blindly down those maze-like corridors and although I had succeeded in shaking off the foot-steps I had almost certainly identified as Jeannie Deveron's, I was also further away from finding Fraser than ever.

Occasionally I stopped in my blind flight, whispered into the gloom: 'Fraser?' I was scared to raise my voice, because she knew the geography of the castle so well and would undoubtedly already be on my tracks.

'Fraser?' A note of desperation, of hysteria, was creeping into my voice—how glad she would be to realise that my nerve was going. I stopped, tried to gather my wits and I began slowly to unwind from the maze-pattern of the corridors. Right, right, right again.

Outside the windows the high trees gleamed. The storm had died and the sun was setting in a glory of faded rose and throwing patterns of colour through the stained glass on to the panelled walls. Strange fascinating colours, if I had had time to stop and

144

admire, patterns of fleur-de-lis, of lions and roses.

I turned a corner and found myself at the top of a spiral stair.

'Fraser?' I whispered. There were footsteps. 'Fraser?' This time my voice was louder, hopeful. The steps slithered into silence. 'Fraser.'

Bang, bang, bang—they were close now, unnervingly close, and I began to run down the stairs.

Down, down—suddenly it was like a film in reverse, a film I had seen before and recently. I jerked to a standstill and only just in time, for the stairs crumbled, petered out into nothing. Sickeningly far below was the overgrown vegetation that surrounded the castle. The night air was cold on my face.

I leaned back weakly against the stone, gathering breath and my remaining strength for the climb back up the stairs into the castle.

Suddenly I listened. Surely—surely I had heard something moving close at hand.

Listen. I tried holding my breath, praying that my heart wouldn't thud so loudly, deafening all exterior sounds.

Listen.

And then I heard it again. A faint slither of footsteps. Close at hand ...

A heavy step ...

Arms seized me from behind. I saw a man's wrists and forearms.

Expecting Fraser, I turned, murmuring his name.

Then I screamed in earnest, for the face, beloved as it was, was not the one I expected to see and being so completely out of context scared me out of the remainder of my wits.

'Candida, what the devil are you doing?' he demanded sternly, 'rushing about all over the place and screaming like a madwoman?'

He had black hair and the kind of light blue eyes that seem an anachronism in so dark a countenance. Eyebrows black and glossily beautiful arched over them and his mouth might have been sculpted by Michaelangelo. Day-dreaming about him, I had nevertheless forgotten how astonishingly handsome was the reality. He had the kind of looks that paled the brightest stars . . .

I rested my head against his shoulder, scared to speak in case the whole scene might vanish.

'Look at me,' he demanded. Slowly I opened my eyes, and there he was, arms outstretched holding me, rescuing me from heavens knows what kind of terrors. Perfectly on cue, he had appeared like every girl's hero, just in the nick of time.

I had prayed for a miracle—even a tiny one—and here he was.

'Ben,' I croaked. 'Ben—what are you doing here?'

And even as I asked, I might have used my senses earlier. That car was exactly the kind he would hire. And hadn't I recognised his voice, calling me across the hall. Why hadn't I had enough confidence in my-self to possibly imagine that he might come to Deveron for me?

'Candy darling, I've come to take you home.'

He kissed me and his lips felt strong and tender, ardent as they had been in our better days together. He held me admiringly at arm's length. 'How good to see you. Dearest girl, what on earth have you been up to?'

The words were enchanting. He had called me 'dearest girl' and 'darling'. Such endearments sent my mind fleeing along paths, all of which ended in scenes of monstrous romanticism, absurdly tender reconcilia-tions. In a moment he would be telling me Debbie meant nothing to him, she had returned home to the States—she hated the British climate, was spoilt and rich and he had been quite, quite wrong about her—it would be exactly like the best of all my fantasies.

'Didn't you hear me calling to you? You always seemed to be running in the opposite direction. Come along, this way.' He wrinkled his nose at the dark corridor at the top of the staircase. 'What a dump,' he whispered. 'Don't tell me this is the temple of glory that Fraser Deveron raved about?'

I felt a moment's loyalty and indignation on behalf of Fraser who was trying so hard to save his castle.

'Didn't I warn you that he was a complete charlatan,' said Ben, distinctly crowing now.

'He's nothing of the kind,' I said angrily. 'Since he inherited from his father, when he was still a boy, he has devoted his entire life to saving Deveron. He's sincere and dedicated . . .'

Ben shook his head. 'You could have fooled me.'

Then I remembered that he was referring to the old man I had just found dead and I explained hurriedly my grim discovery in the Murder Field. The drama of it didn't particularly surprise Ben. He shook his head sadly.

'Didn't I tell you? I knew immediately that he was a phoney. I've got an eye for character—you should trust my judgement, Candida,' he added reproachfully. 'I am hardly ever wrong, you know. No, no, dear, not that way. You're going to end up going round in circles.' And as we emerged into the Great Hall I looked at him with unstinting admiration.

'How did you manage that? You are clever—I got lost for hours the first time I was in here—and just now, before you found me.'

Ben sighed deeply and his smile contained an ingredient I had been slow to recognise until now. It was weary tolerance. 'But then, Candy love, you never did have the slightest sense of direction, did you? Absolutely none at all, even in a built-up area with streets which had names on them, you could get hopelessly lost going from east to west.' He waved a hand airily in the direction from which we had emerged. 'These corridors are built on a simple pattern—left in, right out. My dear girl, I remember rescuing you in hysterics rather too often from the maze in the amusement park at Aynley. And as for all the times you have been supposedly map-reading in the car and I've found myself ten miles further down the road with you in a daydreaming stupor, letting all the signposts flash past . . .' He hugged me close to his side and smiled. 'Never mind, it's part of your charm—I forgive you.'

I hugged him in return, genuinely delighted at the stroke of luck that had brought him back to me. 'Wait —would you like to see the master bedroom where I slept last night? It's over here—and it's rather beautiful,' I added, opening the door.

'The master bedroom, eh.' He looked around critically, frowning and sniffing the air.

'Isn't it gorgeous?' He was silent. 'You do like it, don't you?'

'Mmm. Bit damp, isn't it?' He dragged at the bed curtains. 'Should have got rid of all these moth-eaten drapes long ago. What an unhygienic place to sleep.'

I looked around again, trying to see it with fresh eyes. 'But I thought—I mean, I think it's a lovely room. I asked to sleep here, Ben.'

'Alone?' He turned and regarded me sharply.

'Of course.'

'I just wondered,' he said moodily, tapping his fingers on the bedpost.

'You wondered what?'

'Your attraction at Deveron.' His tone was light, his eyes gleaming.

'If you mean the real Fraser Deveron, then you're quite wrong. He doesn't attract me in the slightest. He's a very nice kind young man, that's all. And he's also very honourable . . .'

'All right, all right—no need to get on your high-horse. I was only asking. You can hardly blame me for wondering. After all, you're hardly experienced in the ways of the wide wicked world and when I heard you calling him, I did rather wonder . . .'

'I only called Fraser—I thought you were him.'

'Really. Then he would have been enchanted to have heard you. He missed a treat.'

'What on earth are you talking about, Ben? I was calling for help.'

'So you were, my dear, so you were. Your exact words could have been open to misinterpretation. They were, if I may remind you, something like this: "Fraser—I'm in the master bedroom. Come, as I have something to show you".'

'I wanted to tell him about Great-Uncle—take him to the Murder Field.'

Ben's smile was sweet, it was also patient disbelief. 'Do you fancy this Fraser?'

'Of course I don't.'

'Are you absolutely sure your great-uncle wasn't just dead drunk?'

'Absolutely. I do know the difference,' I added with dignity. 'I also have my suspicions that he might have been murdered and put there—hidden away in this ready-made grave. Judging by the scarcity of traffic in that region, family curses and the like, he could have stayed there until the last trump . . .'

'Oh what nonsense, Candy. There you go again, over-dramatising everything. Dead he maybe is, but murdered? Why should anyone want to murder him? He seemed a harmless soul, a bit potty, but that's hardly grounds for murder.'

'Why should he be dead in the middle of a field then?'

'Because he probably used the place as a secret liquor store and was a solitary drinker. Besides, if it was stolen booze, he probably felt safer that way. Then one night he just passed quietly away.' He led me to the door. 'Let's get out of here, shall we? A terribly depressing place, a wonder they don't just tear it down and be done with it. I'm afraid these old castles give me the creeps. Fancy anyone idealising them, wanting to live in such gloom and despondency these days. Can you imagine it?' He shivered delicately. 'Think of trying to heat the place, or to entertain one's friends to a civilised meal. I imagine whatever kitchens exist are in the bowels of the basement and every repast, however frugal, is stone-cold by the time it's elevated up two flights of stairs.'

'If you didn't come to see Deveron, why did you come?'

'What a question. I came for you, of course.'

'Why? I thought you were busy—otherwise, just now.'

He regarded me rather shamefaced. 'Well, I was rather worried about you.' He wagged an admonishing finger at me. 'I know only too well what you're like, dear girl, you have absolutely no judgement whatever of people. And quite frankly when I heard via Mrs. Moody that your great-uncle was somehow implicated in your scheme, I smelt a rat at five hundred miles. The old boy was quite ga-ga, you know, but neither you nor my darling momma could see wood for tartan. Anyway, as I was in Scotland it seemed the obvious thing to do.'

'What were you doing in Scotland—when did you arrive?'

He looked uncomfortable. 'The weather has been hellish in York since Debbie arrived. And when she decided that the forecasts were better north of the border she thought she would like to visit Edinburgh to see an old aunt. So we flew up and, quite candidly, I could see after the first hour that the visit was going to be quite dire. A real bore, with family photos and all that jazz—and a maelstrom of rather tedious remote cousins converging on us from the Highlands and the Lowlands.' he paused. 'Well, I thought of my little Candida all alone in Deveron and decided to stage a one-man rescue.' He squeezed my arm. 'Pleased?' he asked, smiling.

'Delighted.'

'Ah, I thought you might be.' And leaning over he kissed me again, while my busy mind galloping ahead detected, without the faintest encouragement, a small cooling in his relations with Debbie—a quarrel even—for Ben hated being bored or being dutiful. I gave him a sidelong look of absolute adoration. Perhaps even at this moment he was considering—no, no, I mustn't think of it. I must wait and see, let him surprise me.

'It was darling of you to come all this way for me.' And as Debbie's name still managed to get stuck in my throat I added : 'Doesn't *she* mind?'

'Debbie?' He thrust back his head and regarded me archly. 'My dear infant, Debbie is the most broad-minded of girls. She certainly doesn't object to you in the slightest, she's much too generous. Actually she does feel terrible about the whole thing and she is most anxious that I should still take my duty seriously of watching over you—in an avuncular way, of course,' he added hastily. 'When I mentioned coming to Deveron, she just said: "Ben, you do that. Go and bring her home to us, the poor dear child." '

The poor dear child felt faintly queasy.

'You see,' Ben continued, 'She's had long long talks with both Rona and myself about her greatest desire, which is not to usurp your position as daughter of the house in any way. She wants everything to continue as it was before and you must stay in the house and live with us . . .'

A kind of bleary outline had slid over the landscape beyond the windows, not only because of the fine rain which had arrived in time to drown the sunset. I closed the bedroom door and followed him across the Great Hall.

'You still haven't told me what made you come here in the first place—I thought you were looking at a cottage in the Inverness direction for Momma.'

So, I explained about the wallet. How I had left it in the woollen mill—I said it was when I was looking at purses suitable for Rona. I would keep the beautiful sweater as a surprise, for the *pièce de résistance*. In case all else failed, that lovely expensive gift could hardly fail to move him.

He ruffled my hair absent-mindedly. 'Just like you to miss the bus.'

He hadn't been listening. 'I didn't miss the bus. I left my wallet . . .'

He shrugged elegantly. 'Oh well, my dear, trust you to behave in your usual daffy-minded fashion, whichever way it was,' he added with a yawn.

Like one who sees the truth written clearly and undeniably, the experience was painful and bitter. And

I wondered how many other conversations he had listened to in the past with that vague sweet and wholly tolerant smile—and never heard a single word.

'I hope you can come back now. Where's your case? I don't want to stay in this dump and I expect you're keen to get home. You must be missing Rona and Aynley House after this life in the wilderness.'

'Perhaps I ought to stay, seeing that I found Great-Uncle. There may be something I can do, and, honestly, I do think there was something very odd about the whole business.'

'Rubbish. You don't have to do anything but sign a statement.' He looked at me sternly. 'I hope you aren't entertaining sentimental ideas about staying for the funeral...'

'Well, I am his only kin,' I admitted weakly.

'Oh, for goodness' sake, Candy. You only knew him for a few weeks in which he sponged off Rona and told you both a pack of lies. I fail to see the need for obligation or sentiment in such circumstances.' He sighed. 'However, if you insist on staying, I'm afraid it will have to be without me. I really can't spare the time...'

He was interrupted by a car engine starting outside with a noisy crashing of gears. Rushing to the window, he stared down and shouted:

'Someone's pinching my car. What a bloody nerve —a woman driver too ... Come on ...'

I looked out quickly and there was Jeannie in the driving seat, the Rolls bouncing and staggering, leaping about the lane like a frightened horse. By the time we reached the castle door she was well past the caravan, the car dodging crazily from side to side with clouds of smoke pouring from its exhaust like an uneasy dragon hunting its prey.

'Who is she?' panted Ben.

'Jeannie Deveron.'

'The old girl I met on the way in? What the devil is she up to? I thought she was the housekeeper and when I asked for the laird of Deveron she went all nervous and speechless and darted away. I thought then she was a bit ga-ga and now I know.'

The car had vanished from sight, only the melody of crashing gears lingered in the night air.

'Tell me,' said Ben angrily, 'are they all like this in Deveron? Or is this just a fragment of the native wit and humour?' He quickened his pace. 'Come along, we'll catch up with her, she won't travel far the way she's driving. I only hope we don't come on a mass of twisted metal before we reach the police station to inform them of the theft.'

'Police station. Oh, Ben, there isn't one at Deveron. It's miles away at Muldoune Bridge.'

'Listen.' Ben seized my arm. 'Hear that?'

It was undoubtedly a car and this time being driven with some confidence. Jeannie Deveron had improved...

Suddenly there was a squeal of brakes and silence.

'My damned car—she's gone and crashed it.'

Together we raced down the lane.

14

In the ditch near Jeannie Deveron's cottage two cars nestled, their bonnets close together. The scene at first glance appeared to be frighteningly still. Imagination raced ahead to twisted metal and broken bodies. The Rolls and, partly hidden by its bulk, the red Volkswagen Fraser had driven on that magic visit into the hills when we had watched the golden eagle. Only two days ago, it already seemed to belong to a safe and almost forgotten world where all was serene and happy.

I began to run towards the red car, shouting: 'Fraser—Fraser.'

Its door swung open, the driver's seat empty. Rusty stretched out on the back seat, wagged her tail at me with grave unconcern.

'Fraser.' And his head bobbed up from the other side of the limousine where he was trying to open the door, to extract Jeannie, whom I now saw slumped over the wheel.

'Is she badly hurt?'

'I don't think so. I wouldn't be surprised if she took a bad turn before she hit the ditch. It gave me quite a turn, because when she appeared, the car was going like something from the dodgems, I thought there was no driver. She must have passed out . . .'

'What about you?'

He smiled. 'I'm all right. I saw her coming and took evasive action.' He looked beyond me at Ben, and waited politely.

When I introduced them Ben nodded briefly, shrugging aside such pleasantries as inappropriate to the time. 'My car,' he demanded, and ignoring our concern for the still figure inside, he said: 'That crazy old woman, she stole it.'

Fraser continued his efforts to wrench open the door. 'Ah, that's it. Jeannie . . .' and he began slapping her hands: 'Jeannie.'

'Is the car badly damaged?' asked Ben.

'We'll soon find out. First things first. Let's see how badly the driver's damaged.'

'Driver indeed, that madwoman.'

A groan indicated Jeannie was coming round. Fraser spoke to her reassuringly. She stirred, looked at him. 'Are you all right?' he asked.

'What happened?'

'I'll help you out. Swing your legs over. That's the way—Now, any bones broken?'

Jeannie stood up gingerly, shook her head and began to totter unsteadily towards her garden gate.

'Oh, my knee—I must have bashed it. No—nothing broken though, I don't think so, Mr. Fraser. I haven't driven a car for thirty years—and it just ran away with me.'

'Really,' said Ben. 'You could have fooled me, I thought you ran away with the car.'

She turned and stared as if she hadn't noticed him before. 'Is there going to be awful trouble for me over this? I'm sorry, sir, I didn't mean any harm.'

'Don't cry,' said Fraser. 'We'll get you inside and you can tell us all about it. There, there—come along, lean on me.' I ran to his side and he looked past me at Ben. 'I could do with your help to get her upstairs, do you mind?'

Ben came forward grudgingly from his inspection of the front of the car. 'How the hell am I going to explain all this? It's a hired car, you know, and damned expensive from Edinburgh.'

Jeannie groaned again and the two men supported her into the cottage, while I followed them upstairs and into her bedroom.

'You'll be all right now,' said Fraser, gently lifting

her on to the bed. 'You lie down quietly for a little while and we'll look after you,' he said soothingly, as if he spoke to a small child. 'Candida will get you a nice cup of tea.'

'And Ben will get you a nice summons,' said my ex-fiancé acidly.

Fraser gave him a sharp look. 'No need for that, surely. Jeannie didn't mean to do your car any harm. It was just an impulsive action.'

'Charming,' said Ben. 'I hope she doesn't give way to such impulses often.'

'I think we'd better hear her explanation before we decide what we're going to do,' said Fraser, whose glance at me indicated clearer than any words that if this was my beloved then my taste in men left much to be desired. He turned his attention back to the woman on the bed. 'How are you now?'

'I'm fine, Mr. Fraser. And you're being far too kind to me. I think I took a blackout, when I started driving the car and saw you coming up the lane. I was sure I was going to run straight into you and when I swerved I don't remember anything more. I must have passed out. My goodness, I've hardly ever fainted in my whole life.'

'I'll go down to the village and get Dr. Archie to take a look at you.'

She seized his arm. 'No, Mr. Fraser, I'd rather not. Please don't bother about me, because I'm perfectly all right—and, you see, I just don't want anyone else to know, especially in the village, what happened.' She looked around wildly and began to cry. 'I don't know what came over me, really I don't. I just had to get away.'

'Away from whom, Jeannie?' asked Fraser gently.

She darted a look at Ben and me. 'Well, you see, I lost my nerve when Miss Brent found the old man's body. Then this other man arrived and I guessed they were in it together. And I got scared . . .'

'You've found old Jamie?' Fraser whispered to me. I nodded and he indicated that we adjourn outside the bedroom, where with Ben listening grim and silent, apart from registering occasional contributions of contempt mingled with concern for the fate of his car, I explained briefly my grim discovery in the Murder Field.

When I had finished Ben's impatience exploded in a keen desire to go outside and minister to the needs of his wounded vehicle.

'How about a cup of tea first?' asked Fraser pleasantly.

'Don't be insulting,' said Ben. 'What I need is a stiff brandy.'

'There's some whisky in the kitchen cupboard in the caravan,' said Fraser. 'It's the best I can do at short notice, but by all means go and help yourself.'

'Please don't trouble on my account, I dare say I'll survive. Who knows, with a bit of luck, if we can get this business over and done with in the next hour, we might still be in time for the bar to be open at the local. I think we'll all have earned a drink.'

'In that case, perhaps you'll bear with us a little longer,' said Fraser politely. 'Let's go down to the kitchen and while Candida brews us a pot of tea, we can decide what I'm to tell the police.'

'The truth, I hope,' said Ben piously, 'as I shall tell them.'

'Poor Jeannie,' I said.

'Poor all of us,' said Ben.

158

Fraser looked solemn. 'Yes, I suppose Jeannie's behaviour was undoubtedly that of someone with something to hide.'

'You mean she did the old man in and hid him,' said Ben. 'Now that's a splendid feat of imagination.' He chuckled. 'You must read the same kind of books as Candida here, full of superhuman heros and unquenchable villains. Now, as I remember the old man he must have weighed about seventeen stones and from what Candy has told us, she could hardly keep on an even keel walking over the blighted heath. If that's the case, how would it be for an elderly woman to negotiate dragging a dead and very heavy man behind her?'

Fraser ignored him. 'Unfortunately the police have had suspicions of foul play for a while now. Once the snow melted from the upper reaches of Cairn Dever, they were afraid that if Jamie had been murdered, then the murderer might try to get to the body first and destroy any evidence. Another thing was that Jeannie claimed to be the last person to see him alive. According to her, they exchanged words outside the cottage on the fatal day he disappeared. Anyway, the county police have had a lively interest in the case and a few days ago they thought the helicopter spotted something. As I knew the mountain well, they roped me in some time ago to give them a hand. Alas, all our digging revealed was a deer carcase, part buried in snow and very human looking, I can assure you, from above, veiled in slight mist.'

'Was that yesterday morning when I saw you coming up the lane at five o'clock carrying a spade?'

'Don't be irrelevant, Candida,' said Ben sternly, 'let him get on with his story.'

Fraser looked at me as if Ben hadn't interrupted. 'Yes, I was hoping to be unobtrusive at the time. I didn't want you mentioning it to anyone—I was under strict instructions to keep quiet my part in the county police's little drama.'

'At least I'm relieved to know I *did* see you and that you weren't part of my other hallucinations that night.'

'Hallucinations,' murmured Ben. 'I'll be seeing pink elephants if someone doesn't get something decided soon.'

'I'm most reluctant to have the police interview Jeannie about the car just now, Mr. Armstrong, especially considering the sequence of events. Candida discovering old Jamie and so on. I'm very fond of the old lady and I'd like to talk to her first, prepare her—find out, if I can, what really happened. Whatever it was, I think she's so frightened now that she'll tell me the truth. Now, how's about the tea?'

'No thanks,' said Ben, 'I've just given it up. If you'll excuse me,' and he disappeared impatiently towards the car.

When I took the tea upstairs on a tray, Fraser was heaping pillows behind Jeannie. He put milk and sugar into her cup and sat on the bed while she drank it. 'Now when you've finished that, we'll have a little talk.'

When she put down her cup I took it as a signal for my departure.

'No, no, Mr. Fraser, I'd like the young lady to stay. I'd like the gentleman to hear it too. Perhaps they might understand what made me do it,' she added with dignity.

A car started up outside and the engine gave forth

an ominous rattle. I followed Fraser to the window in time to see Ben step out of the car with a face like thunder. He came upstairs.

'Besides the wing being bashed, the silencer's broken. I can hardly limp back to Edinburgh in this condition. Can I get it fixed—is there somewhere here, where I can get it done tonight?'

Fraser nodded absently. 'Can we hear first of all what Jeannie has to say?' He smiled at the woman in the bed. 'Go ahead.'

She looked in mute appeal at Ben, then at me. 'I don't know why I stole the gentleman's car, except that I thought in some way I was helping Joe, delaying things in a way. I saw you in the Murder Field, Miss Brent, and then when the gentleman arrived—you, sir, I was sure you were a plain-clothes policeman and had come to arrest me. That's why I ran away.'

Ben drew himself to his full height. 'I can assure you, madam, that to imagine me in the role of plain-clothes man, detective, inspector or Sherlock Holmes, is a supreme piece of mis-casting. My feet are not nearly big enough and, I can assure you, my suits cost a great deal more than those worn by plain-clothes policemen,' he added, sounding distinctly hurt. 'Anyway, why should I want to arrest you?'

She hesitated for a moment, bit her lip. 'Because I expect I'm what is called an accessory. You see,' she continued rapidly, 'old Jamie the night before he—disappeared—had a quarrel with my boy Joe. He used to get nasty when he was drunk—and very threatening. I'd been to a church meeting at the village and when I came home Joe said: "I've done it now, he won't threaten us again." He said he had been coming home across the Murder Field when Jamie jumped out of—that place—where he hid his stolen whisky and accused Joe of spying on him and trying to steal his bottles. There was a fight. Joe said Jamie fell and he realised he must have killed him, so he pushed him in the little cave and said nobody would find him there, at least not for a long time. Then poor Joe, he cried, because he didn't want to kill the old man and the police would be after him and everything. So I said I'd help him to escape. I had a letter from him a few weeks later from London saying he had this marvellous chance to start a new life, he was going to send for me. We'd both begin again . . .'

She stopped and began to sob quietly.

'When did you last hear from him, Jeannie?'

She wiped her eyes. 'Nothing, not a word since that last letter.' Then she looked at us, lifted her head proudly and, voice defiant, said: 'But I believe in my boy. He'll send for me some day, I know he will.'

In the pause that followed there seemed nothing any of us, even Ben, could say. Then I remembered. 'Was that really a ghostly massacre I heard, the night I stayed here, Mrs. Deveron?' I asked.

She shook her head, avoiding my eyes. 'No, it was a recording—I took it from a battle on a radio play. I thought it would help to keep strangers away. Most of the Deveron folk—and you know this is true, Mr. Fraser—apart from Joe and the old man, wouldn't go across the Murder Field for a pension. There is something there, you know,' she added quietly.

I didn't know. But I was extremely glad that in the last few minutes two of my 'hallucinations' had been explained by natural means. Obviously it was just a question of time before my strange encounters on Cairn Dever and in the secret room with its missing Allan Ramsay portrait were similarly explained.

Ben broke the silence by asking: 'Do you think I can possibly get the car fixed tonight? How long will it take?'

'The garage is closed and tomorrow morning will be the earliest,' said Fraser, a fraction impatiently. 'I must go into Deveron now. And I want Dr. Archie to take a look at you'—he indicated the woman on the bed—'just to make sure, Jeannie. Yes, I *do* insist. No more protests.'

She clutched his arm. 'Will it be all right, Mr. Fraser, sir? I won't be put in hospital or anything like that—and have to miss the wedding? Morna's relying on me to make her dress—and I've the wedding cake to bake too.'

'You have two weeks, Jeannie,' he whispered, and watching as they smiled at each other, I felt suddenly cast out, hurt and offended beyond measure that I hadn't been told about the wedding before. And obviously the slight pressure of Fraser's hands on Jeannie's could be taken as a gesture of warning, and a signal that I wasn't to be included in the secret now. As we left her, I darted a reproachful look at Fraser's happy countenance, wanting to say something, but the appropriate words got stuck in my throat.

Suddenly Ben's acid comment removed my murmured 'congratulations' blankly received by Fraser into other realms: 'Couldn't you use your *droit de seigneur* or whatever it is, to conjure up a mechanic straightaway?'

'I'll do my best. But at least let me offer you the hospitality of Devron for tonight,' said Fraser.

He could afford to be magnanimous, I thought, and

163

Morna somewhat reckless too, with the wedding day fixed and Max Craig out of the way. I hoped they all knew quite clearly what they were doing.

'Exactly what had you in mind?' asked Ben sweetly, with just a suspicion of rudeness in his tone.

'Well, there is a bed already made up in the castle —and a fire going too.' Fraser surprisingly included us both in his smile, until I remembered that he thought Ben and I, engaged and probably lovers already, would relish such a prospect. I must have looked slightly shocked, for he added awkwardly: 'One can always put a camp-bed in the dressing-room next door, of course.'

'I rather think not,' said Ben icily. 'Actually Candida and I will be as comfortable as can reasonably be expected in the local hotel if you would care to drop us off. I don't suppose Devron has a taxi service.'

Fraser smiled. 'It would be as easy for me to take you, especially as neither Jeannie nor I have the telephone installed.'

Ben groaned and lifted his eyes to heaven, indicating that such lack of civilities was very clearly The End.

'The nearest hotel is at Muldoune Bridge.'

'Good grief, man, that place again. I'm beginning to hate the sound of it. Does the cradle of civilisation in these parts begin and end at Muldoune Bridge?'

Fraser smiled patiently. 'I'm going in there anyway, so I'll be glad to give you a lift.'

'Ah well,' said Ben, 'at least there is a police station.'

We were both silent at that. He shuffled his feet a bit at our reproachful looks and said: 'I gather you'll both think I'm an absolute monster if I do anything now to get this crazy woman into trouble.'

Fraser's silence was eloquent. I said: 'Poor Mrs. Deveron—you heard her story, Ben. Don't you think she's suffered enough?'

'My dear girl, law and order must be maintained, wrongdoers must be punished even when they happen to be our nearest and dearest. If we let people off who steal cars on impulse, where on earth will it all end?'

'Look,' said Fraser, 'if there has to be a scapegoat, then let it be me. I'll take the blame. I skidded in the VW—which was quite true—the road was muddy. You can say that you had to leap into the ditch to avoid me. I'll settle from my insurance and pay for your repair. How about that? Does that satisfy you?'

Ben sniffed. 'Oh very well,' he said with a bored yawn. 'I can afford to play your little game of chivalry, outdated as it is. But I still warn you that you shouldn't let her get away with it. And for heaven's sake don't bother to pay for the repair. Let's be magnanimous— a few pounds won't matter.' He smiled, striving, alas, too late, for the full impact of the old charming manner that had trapped so many unsuspecting clients in the past history of Perseus Plastics. 'A few pounds— it's nothing, nothing at all. The only thing is that I do have moral principles, I don't fancy protecting a criminal.'

'Criminal?' asked Fraser. 'We can't decide that until we hear the procurator fiscal's report. After all, whatever Joe said—and he's a daft young lad who was terrified out of his wits—Jamie was old, he did drink too much and it was well known that he did have a bad heart.'

As we approached the VW, Rusty, who had been minding her own business in the back all this time, suddenly stamped out of the car as Fraser opened the door. She paddled her feet in a great puddle and then with shrieks of welcome launched herself, muddy paws and all, on Ben. Unprepared for this onslaught, Ben stumbled backwards and was at once up to his ankles in the muddy ditch. All this was adding insult to injury, for Ben was not well known as a dog-lover by even normal domestic standards. He tolerated clients' pets as a necessary evil of business, to be avoided, like their children, on every possible occasion.

And there was Rusty greeting him like an old friend, barking with delight, tail wagging at crescendo, muddy paws embracing him. Fraser, rendered speechless at this spectacle of low comedy, called her to heel too late to repair the holocaust that had overtaken Ben.

Ben was furious and concealed it badly, attacking his suit with an elegant white hanky. Fraser was furious too and attacked Rusty with a none-too-gentle hand. Rusty adopted a whipped-cur attitude and slunk back into the car, regarding us all with the utmost dejection.

Fraser apologised. 'I can't imagine what came over her. She never does things like that. I just can't understand it. She must have taken a fancy to you.'

Ben grunted angrily and I said : 'Yes, she is always so well behaved.'

Ben snorted. 'And what might you know about it? You've only seen the dog for a couple of days. Of course, your judgement can't be taken seriously,' he said rudely, 'anything on four legs and you're quite daft about it.'

I sat down beside Rusty, who kept her eyes demurely

lowered. She was all contrition, yet as I moved her along the seat she gave me what almost amounted to a wink of conspiracy. If a dog could be said to give anyone an old-fashioned look, she actually grinned. I restrained my amusement with some difficulty. The behaviour of Rusty was so completely out of character one would readily have suspected—in a dog less thoroughbred—that she had misbehaved herself with Ben out of motives of spite.

15

While we waited for Fraser outside the doctor's surgery, Ben said: 'Please don't sulk, Candida, there's a good girl.'

'I'm not sulking—I'm just being quiet,' I answered from my seat in the back of the car.

'I'm relieved to hear it. I thought maybe I was dragging you unwillingly away from Deveron. You should know my feelings about the quaint and the picturesque by now. Their charms are completely lost on me unless they include one hundred per cent efficiency. After all I've been through today I don't feel like spending the night in a grotty old castle—Gothic ruins I find neither romantic nor enchanting, especially if I am expected to sleep in them. I like my comforts, thank you . . .'

At that moment Fraser returned and said: 'Dr. Archie is going over to have a look at Jeannie. Next port of call, the Keirs' garage. You'd better come along and add your persuasion,' he added to Ben.

I watched them talking to Morna's father, two men utterly different. Ben so handsome and elegant, looking as if he had stepped from the pages of a glossy magazine advertising what the well-dressed man was wearing this season—the ravages of Rusty's muddy paws and his encounter with the muddy ditch were not evident at this distance.

Then Fraser with his red hair, his jeans and sweater. Suddenly it seemed that the roles they played were all wrong. Ben should have been cast as the young laird, with a gun tucked under his arm, his arrogance belonged to an eighteenth-century painting by Gainsborough. Fraser had the face of a warrior lord, a fighter. He belonged in some other time, with Bruce and Wallace and Bannockburn, where men fought for causes more stirring and glorious than keeping a roof on a castle.

Ben began to look pleased. I could see him laying on the charm inches thick when Morna came to the door. They were introduced and I observed that she was also impressed by this newcomer. It didn't really surprise me, for there was a certain similarity between Ben Armstrong and Max Craig.

She noticed me in the car and waved, smiling, her action indicating that Fraser must have explained my peculiar experiences in the castle and that she had forgiven my strange behaviour towards her. An odd girl, in many ways mature beyond her years. From what Mrs. Deveron had told me—confirmed by Fraser himself—the Deveron men were somewhat naive in choosing wives. If there was a lack of enthusiasm in my response to Morna's greeting it was due to my doubts whether she would make Fraser happy.

Ben returned to the car wearing the jaunty air that declared itself so often in other surroundings as the successful conclusion of some particular tricky business deal.

'That's all right, is it, then?' asked Fraser, as he drove off, blowing a kiss to Morna, as we went.

'Splendid,' said Ben with a sigh, relaxing in his seat.

'What happened?'

'Mr. Keir will get his mechanic to fix it first thing tomorrow and have it at the hotel ready for us when we leave.'

'You'll have to come back to Deveron tonight, Candida,' Fraser interrupted. 'The county police want a statement about your discovering the body. Just routine, of course.'

Ben made an uncomplimentary noise.

'It shouldn't take long,' said Fraser soothingly. 'They'll be at Deveron directly and, of course, I shall still drive you over to the hotel at Muldoune Bridge.' He looked at Ben. 'If you like, I can drop you there now and drive Candida over later.'

'No, no. I suppose I had better come along too and see her there safely,' said Ben, in tones suggesting that he was used to treating me like a five-year-old child and backward at that.

We met Dr. Archie leaving Jeannie's cottage. 'She's fine, nothing to worry about, but it's always as well to make sure.'

'Come along to the caravan with us?' asked Fraser.

'No, thanks,' said the doctor. 'I'm afraid I'm still on the job.' And, pointing down the lane. 'There's the police car and the ambulance now, hot on our heels.'

I was introduced to Inspector Miles as the dead man's great-niece who had accidentally discovered his body, and Dr. Archie said: 'Mrs. Deveron won't mind if you chat in her cottage, by the way. I've given her something to make her sleep,' he added to the inspector. 'She got a terrible shock, the old man being so near all this time. She has a bad heart, you know,' he explained blandly. There was no mention of the limousine's part in this little drama. It was parked up near the caravan, looking peaceful and contented— and reasonably whole. As Dr. Archie followed the policeman across the Murder Field, I guessed he knew the whole story and the real reason for Jeannie's collapse, but guessed also that Deveron would protect Deveron to the last ditch.

Ben adjourned to the caravan with Fraser while I sat in Jeannie's living room and signed an official statement. I gave them my address in York, but when they supposed politely that I might be staying at Deveron for the funeral, I murmured: 'I expect so.' simply because I felt foolishly that any other decision from their point of view might seem suspicious.

As we left the cottage, Ben and Fraser, who must have been keeping a look-out, came down the lane in the car. The journey to Muldoune Bridge was so silent I wondered what had been the conversation between the two men in my absence. When we reached our destination it was to find that the only hotel hadn't a room left.

Fraser pointed out innumerable bed-and-breakfast establishments along the road, but these were scorned by Ben, who refused to countenance overnight accommodation which did not also include a private bathroom.

Anxiously I regarded the back of Fraser's head as patiently he switched on the light to study the A.A. handbook. 'There are several hotels within a radius of ten miles or so. How does this one sound?' He read out the details. 'Shall we try it?'

'Excellent, excellent—please take us there if it isn't too much trouble,' said Ben.

Reflected lights from approaching cars on the road illuminated Fraser as a dark shadow disembodied and unreal. I was horribly aware that Ben was already treating him in 'my-good-man' fashion, as if he was a paid chauffeur. I only hoped that Fraser had a sense of humour. My own feelings were shame at Ben's behaviour, especially as I realised that Fraser had ceased directing any remarks to me for some time. I was doubtless included in Ben's disgrace by association and had I been able to read his mind I felt sure I would have seen considerable eagerness to rid himself of his unwelcome cargo.

Wistfully I wondered if his irritation allowed any room for the realisation that in a few moments we would both be going our separate ways and quite unlikely ever to meet again. And if he did know, did he care at all?

I found myself remembering the happy hours we had spent together. It did seem sad that it should end like this, with Fraser's predominant memory of how glad he had been to get rid of his remote English relative. After all, with a rather deplorable English mother and a randy English grandmother, he had little reason to be predisposed towards the female of the English species. I could picture myself—and Ben—as the fascinated topic of conversation between Morna and himself.

Suddenly the journey seemed endless. I wanted it to

be over with as little inconvenience as possible. Not that such would restore me to any tenderness in Fraser's remembrances, but because I was sure he now had a lasting impression that I was a tiresome silly girl with a particularly unendearing pompous fiancé.

Sensing the antagonism existing between the two men, I wished it could have been different. Why couldn't they have liked each other, then Ben would have been willing to help Fraser financially to restore the castle and the glen. Perhaps at some future date all three of us—no, four, including Morna—could have enjoyed a rewarding friendship for the rest of our lives. Since Ben had reappeared I was naively hopeful —my optimism for a future that included him had revived considerably. Certain that Ben would never have gone out of his way to come to Deveron for me unless he was really concerned, I felt rather triumphant that Debbie's move in introducing tiresome relatives had been a grave mistake at this juncture of their relationship. She had been guilty of boring him and in no time at all she would disappear back to the States.

The long drive leading to the Victorian mansion which was now an imposing and elegant hotel impressed Ben, so did the well-lit, well-carpeted reception hall, the porter who rushed out for our luggage. Such soothing benefits of civilised living were sufficient to restore him to passable good humour and as we waited to be taken up to our rooms he smiled at Fraser and said :

'All's well that ends well, eh? At least let me offer you a drink for all your trouble.'

Fraser shook his head. 'No trouble at all. Thanks, but it's late and I must be getting back.'

He looked at me. So this was farewell. We stood smiling but awkward in Ben's presence. I thought of all we might have said as he took my hand and murmured that it had been great meeting me. Rather formally I thanked him for his hospitality.

'We must keep in touch,' he said.

'Yes, we must.'

He shook hands briefly with Ben and before I realised he had gone down the steps and out of my life. It was even too dark now to wave goodbye, to watch the little red car drive away.

We had the resident's lounge to ourselves and Ben was disposed to be festive. 'How about a little drink, Candy? A nightcap?'

I shook my head, looking around the walls, heavy with sporting trophies of fish in glass cases, long-departed deer run to moth, wild-cats still realistically snarling, eagles with furry prey. It was all singularly depressing. 'I think I'll go to bed.'

'We haven't had a chance to talk,' he said in wounded tones.

'We'll talk in the car tomorrow. It's been a long day—I'm tired.'

'Very well, I'll see you to your room.'

We climbed the stairs silently and at the end of a long corridor he unlocked my door, kissed me awkwardly on the cheek. As I said good night I just wanted to fall into oblivion. I hadn't the energy to sort out the various emotions that goodnight kiss might have stirred, such as regret. With a sigh, I tumbled into bed. I wanted to forget all about Deveron, but small persistent scenes remained and I lay and thought of all the loose ends, the endings I would never know, although Fraser had promised to keep me informed if he ever found the hidden room and the Allan Ramsay portrait.

I awoke early next morning, had a bath and felt much better. I decided to give Ben the sweater I had bought for him that first day at Muldoune Bridge. I would hand it over before we went down to breakfast together. He could admire it in the privacy of his room and pack it away with his luggage.

'Hello, Candy dear, sleep well? Me, too, like a log. Good news this morning, the garage has just phoned. Mr. Keir got a mechanic out early, they're able to repair the car. It was much less severe than I imagined, thank goodness.'

He was putting on his tie before the mirror and presented a freshly cologned cheek for my kiss. I sat on the bed and watched him as I had done so many hundreds of times in our life at Aynley House I wondered if seeing me there aroused any of the old emotions for him, reminding him also that this moment was like stepping back into a past where we had loved each other in serenity and content, where our future was assured and any idea of parting absurd. As I watched him I found I had forgotten all the small intimacies inseparable from loving a man and living for years under the same roof. I gulped as I found my heart aching again with the renewed sadness of losing him. Sick with panic at a future without him, I was back under the enchanter's spell, willing to forgive him his behaviour to Fraser. No doubt he had had an og day, the end of a series of tiresome and exhausting events with Debbie's relatives in Edinburgh.

After all, Ben Armstrong *was* Ben Armstrong. And when he called the wheels of life moved smoothly, unobtrusively. He wasn't used to being thwarted by the same trivia as the rest of the world, he was too godlike to suffer from the tedium, the normal setbacks that afflicted ordinary mortals. I was aware of his eyes regarding me through the mirror with amusement.

'And what are you concealing so inexpertly behind your back?'

Proudly I produced the sweater, regretting that it wasn't more of a surprise in its polythene bag, for the elegant box which would have been a lovely overture was so battered I had left it behind.

'Oh—and who is that for? Rona?'

'No,' I said in shocked tones. 'It's for you, of course.'

'For me? A present from you, Candy?' He sounded astonished, which augured well. 'Well, thank you, dear.' But he made no move to take it and went on brushing his hair.

'Don't you want to try it on?'

Laughing, he turned to me. 'Later, darling. We're going down to breakfast now.'

'Don't you want to look at it, then?'

'Of course I do.' He seized it and shook it out of its bag rather impatiently. Then he held it up to the light, eyeing it critically in front of his reflection. 'Mmm,' he murmured appreciatively. 'It seems quite nice, doesn't it? And it's the right size. Thank you, dear.' Thrusting it back into the bag, he tossed it to me. 'Catch. Just shove it into my suitcase somewhere, will you, if you can find a corner. Now—are we ready? I'm famished.'

I looked at the sweater. 'You don't like it, do you?'

He put an arm around my shoulders. 'Of course I do. Mind you, that shade of blue isn't my colour this season, I have nothing to wear it with right now, but I may get something later. And anyway,' he flashed me a brilliant smile, 'it's the thought that counts and I do appreciate your little kindness.'

I followed him downstairs wishing I had left on the label, longing to tell him that my 'little kindness' had cost two weeks' salary. Apparently he had even forgotten all the trouble it had started, leaving my wallet in the woollen mill, having me seek refuge penniless at Deveron.

The dining-room was a large and floridly Gothic room, heavy with panelling and its original décor. Rather as if the whole mansion had been bought, lock, stock and antimacassars, from the impoverished laird who was doubtless heartily relieved to be rid of it.

Even the lovely views of hills and loch we had glimpsed coming downstairs was hidden behind bucolic stained-glass windows depicting martyred saints and heroic stanzas from Scottish history. There was a raised dais at one end of the room, occupied by a grand piano, potted palms and a lectern at the ready. As if the manager might have listed the Church among his previous vocations and was ready to leap up and invite us to join in a hymn of praise. Had he done so I felt sure the entire dining-room would have abandoned their bacon-and-eggs for a rendering of the 23rd Psalm.

'You look amused,' said Ben. 'What are you thinking?'

'Nothing really.' At one time I would have told him, eagerly sharing my speculations. But now it was too late. The lines of communication we had once shared were battered and broken, they did not even run along the same track.

'Come along,' he said encouragingly. 'Share the joke. Heaven knows I could use a laugh this morning and being witty at breakfast is one of your rare accomplishments. So few women are at their best first thing in the morning.'

'Sorry, I don't feel witty. I'm rather out of practice in my role as the Armstrong family joker—I've left my cap and bells elsewhere.'

'Your what? Oh, I see.' He laughed. 'Very good, very good. Now let me see,' he said, preparing to humour me. 'Your ill-concealed mirth has something to do with that elderly couple over there in the corner. You've been staring at them. I know, they're not married at all—they're lovers eloping together.'

At one time we might both have laughed at such an incongruous idea. Now I realised I hadn't even seen the couple he indicated.

'Ah—bacon-and-eggs at long last. The comic relief will doubtless be adjourned for the toast,' said Ben.

As we ate I watched the sun, shining through the stained glass behind us, throwing pretty patterns of saints and sinners, armorial bearings and flowers across the white tablecloth.

Ben was looking at his watch. 'The car will be here in a few minutes. Are you ready?'

'It's a gorgeous day, can we explore for a while on the journey back?' I was still waiting for a miracle, certain that all we needed to resurrect a dead love was a few hours on our own.

'I'd love to, nothing better. But, you see, Debbie will be waiting for us in Edinburgh. She's dying to meet you.'

Here was a new dimension to returning to York with Ben. I hadn't even considered the possibility of having Debbie's company all the way from Edinburgh to York and then for however long she was remaining at Aynley House. Miserably I realised all my day-dreams about Debbie being sent back to the States were quite unfounded. She was still very much included in Ben's plans for the future. I saw myself being patted on the head, humoured and generally treated in the patronising manner of a poor relation in a Jane Austen novel. And no one could say Ben hadn't warned me.

My eyes misted over as he prattled on extolling Debbie's virtues and I saw only the shifting colours the stained glass had thrown all around us. Like patterns of a burst bubble that had been my false promises of joy . . .

Ben was saying it was time to go. I trailed after him to the door, watching him pay the bill, saw the porter carry out our luggage. I also caught one or two admiring and envious glances from girls who presumed that Ben was my property. He forged ahead, smiling and confident, carrying briefcase and, sadly crushed in one fist, the polythene bag containing my gift. The sweater wasn't even worth the bother of unlocking his suitcase.

'Candida,' he said sternly, 'haven't you forgotten something?'

I looked down and remembered my shoulder bag still nestling over the back of a dining-room chair. He made a weary long-suffering face and I raced back. The room was empty of diners, the white cloths spartan, and I forgave the hotel everything as the glorious light from the windows had taken over, dyeing every space with the myriad shades of a rainbow gone wild.

I ran through a sea of colour and in the centre of the white cloth at the table where we had breakfasted was a perfectly stylised Jacobite Rose.

The White Rose.

I stood like one possesssed, knowing now why the stained glass had nagged at me all through the meal. Knowing where I had seen a symbol exactly like this one before. When I had been lost in Deveron Castle last night, the sunset glow had cast patterns on the panels of the corridor. Fleur-de-lis—and the white rose.

There must be some significance . . .

Ben was chatting to the Keirs' mechanic, a little truck stood close by, with the driver waiting to take his companion back to Deveron now that the limousine was safely delivered.

'Get in,' said Ben, without turning round. 'We're late enough as it is.'

I went over to the truck and said : 'Excuse me, are you going straight back?'

'To Muldoune Bridge first—I have a call to make there.'

'Will you give me a lift?'

'A tight squeeze, miss, but you're welcome.'

Ben was behind me. 'What's wrong—what's the trouble now?'

'No trouble at all, Ben. I'll see you in York. I'm not coming back to Edinburgh with you. I'm going to Deveron. There's something important I must tell Fraser.

16

As the van drove off I watched Ben's indignant face retreating, hoping the Keirs' mechanic, Jock, hadn't overheard his parting remarks.

Was his accusation true? Was I fooling myself about the real reason for my decision to return to Deveron? I had insisted it was an undeniable sense of obligation to the old man I had met five years ago. However my great-uncle had died, it was shocking to lie unburied for several months, then to be thrust into the grave with no relative to mourn him.

'He was my great-uncle, it's my duty to stay,' I had said to Ben.

'Sentimental twaddle,' he sneered. 'Besides, Fraser will attend to it admirably, have no fears.'

'Why should I sneak off? Fraser has plenty to do. After all, the old man was only a Deveron shepherd, one of his many tenants.'

I wondered whether seeing the shadow of the white rose outlined on the tablecloth in the hotel had stirred these dormant feelings, knowing my great-uncle's pride in race, how deeply he cared about Deveron and its legends, even to a grandiose but harmless pretence to be its laird.

My other reason I had given Ben for returning was nebulous in the extreme, a chance that the panel to the secret room lay in front of the stained-glass window containing a white rose.

In Muldoune Bridge, while Jock selected tyres from the garage, I walked down the street and bought some chocolates for Jeannie. Returning to the van, I thought about my first day here less than a week ago, when I had seen Fraser and Rusty from the bus window and thought how beautifully they belonged to the landscape. Idly I had wished I could know them and that wish had been granted. We had met again here, the three of us, after my *faux pas* with Morna. Ashamed I was running away and Fraser had unceremoniously taken me off the bus and returned me to Deveron to wait until the wallet containing my tickets and money was returned from the mill down the street where I had left it.

I sighed. It was expecting too much of fate that a third encounter could be imminent . . .

I seemed to hear Ben's words: 'Be honest, Candy, your decision has nothing to do with duty or sentiment. You're simply going back because you're in love with Fraser. Come on, admit it. Anyone could see with half an eye how things were between you . . .'

I stopped in my tracks, knowing that something quite miraculous had taken place since my last visit to Muldoune Bridge. I had learnt that time has little to do with falling in—or out—of love. At this moment I knew that all I had felt for Ben throughout five long years had been cancelled in three days. I knew the exact moment I had fallen in love with Fraser, when he kissed me by the river where the deer drank, for Ben Armstrong had never awakened such a tumult in my heart, such fire or longing. Now I realised I had mistaken hero-worship and sisterly affection for love. Fraser, with whom I shared so many things—even the mutual discovery and admiration of a rare poetess—was such an obvious choice of mate.

I sighed. Perhaps I had taken refuge in pretending I was still engaged to Ben because Fraser was another man I couldn't have. By his own admission he had loved Morna for years, and was marrying her in two weeks. The wedding must have been already arranged before my arrival in Deveron. As for Morna's presence at Tillicross, only a combination of circumstances and some ill-directed feminine intuition on my part hinted at an intrigue involving Max Craig. There was probably an innocent explanation, some garage business for her father, but for all I knew, Fraser might be a violently jealous lover, so she remained carefully out of sight.

After all, I knew nothing about Fraser, except that in a brief and passing friendship he had found me attractive enough to kiss one day, merely because time, place and mood had all been right. He had behaved on impulse and probably now regretted it. His subsequent behaviour certainly hadn't suggested it had some deeper meaning or that he considered he was being disloyal to Morna in any way.

If I hadn't led so cloistered a life during my long engagement to Ben I would doubtless have found such kisses on short acquaintance quite normal and acceptable if the climate were right for casual romance. After all, the evidence of his devotion to Morna had never been in any doubt.

I was a silent passenger on the return to Deveron. Committed now to meeting Fraser again, I must do the best I could to hide my real feelings by letting him believe I was still engaged to Ben, I only hoped that he hadn't guessed them as accurately as Ben. Now although pride was a somewhat painful indulgence, I wished Ben knew about Morna, just in case he imagined that since he was out of my orbit, I was quite desperately throwing myself at every eligible man who came along.

I left the van at the garage and walked up the lane.

At Jeannie's cottage a strange young woman came to the door. 'Yes, I'm her niece.' She thanked me profusely for the chocolates and invited me to go upstairs and see her. 'She's much better today, resting, but she'll be glad to see you.' I said I'd come by later and the girl continued: 'It's such a relief to everyone in Deveron to know that old Jamie wasn't murdered. Mr. Fraser was down to tell her as soon as he got the news that it was death from natural causes, a heart attack, they said. Awful, isn't it,' she whispered with a shiver, 'to think of him lying so close all this time. Aye, it'll be another ghost to walk in Murder Field, like as not.'

I hurried on to the caravan, pleased with the verdict and even more pleased to see Fraser's old Land-Rover parked outside. The caravan was empty. Of course, I thought sadly, he was probably at the garage celebrating at the Keirs' house. I looked up at the castle dark and grim, and decided to fill in time until he returned, by playing my hunch. I would search for the stained-glass window with its white rose and hope that it gave some clue to the secret room.

Crossing the Great Hall, I heard Rusty bark. The library door opened and Fraser appeared. He looked so genuinely pleased and, rushing forward, seized my hands with such vigour and delight, for a moment I thought he was going to kiss me again. I stepped back hastily.

'Candida—I thought you'd gone . . .'

Releasing my hands from his grip, I kept a safe distance between us. 'It seemed so cowardly to go without knowing what had really happened to old Jamie. I feel a sense of duty . . .' I continued awkwardly, my pride hoping the real reason wasn't now abundantly clear to him, 'even knowing it was natural causes.

Jeannie's niece told me, when I called at the cottage ...'

'Then you realise it isn't necessary for you to stay. I'll see to everything. It's just a formality now—the funeral will be in a couple of days.'

'I'm so glad Joe didn't murder him, after all.'

'Me too. Particularly for Jeannie's sake. How did you get here, by the way? I thought you'd be half-way to Edinburgh by now.'

'I came in the Keirs' van—begged a lift.'

He reached out and took my hands again. 'It was good of you to come back, Candida. I'm glad you did,' he added shyly.

'I had another reason.'

He lifted his head, asked eagerly : 'And what was that?'

So I told him about seeing the white rose reflected on the tablecloth in the hotel and how it reminded me that there was a white rose in one of the stained-glass windows along the castle's corridors.

'My dear, you could have saved yourself the journey—I mean, you could have written all this in a letter.'

'Yes, I know. Call it vanity, if you like, the desire to say I-told-you-so, I wanted to be here when you find that room—if it exists outside my imagination.'

'You're beginning to have doubts, eh?'

'I'm afraid so.'

Still he didn't move and stood playing with my hands, turning them over, looking at them intently. 'Was that the only reason why you came back, Candida?'

I felt the colour rise to my face in a sudden shaming tide. 'Of course it was.' And angrily I pulled my hands free.

184

It was Fraser's turn to look embarrassed. He walked across to the library table where we had searched the files of newspaper clips for clues. 'As you can see, I haven't given up hope yet. It's worth another look. But before we go, Candida, you must be prepared for disappointment. I could swear no such room exists— secret rooms of any size are more difficult to conceal than the layman might suppose. Besides, if it did exist, surely there would have been rumours about it in the family records. These kind of legends, when based on fact, tend to persist.' He touched the bulky file. I'm sure my father would have known. He did so much research on the family in his invalid years.'

'At least he would be delighted to know it hadn't all been in vain—for if there is an Allan Ramsay, then his ambition, his life's work, would be justified.'

Fraser smiled. 'What are we waiting for then?' he asked softly.

'There's another reason—it would be the perfect wedding present for Morna. "The White Rose of Deveron" who is almost her double.'

'I have no intentions of giving it to Morna. She has nothing to do with it.'

'Well, you are marrying her in a couple of weeks.'

'I am? Now where did you get that idea?'

'From Jeannie Deveron. She said she hoped she wouldn't miss the wedding.'

'Indeed she did—but she wasn't referring to my wedding.'

'But when I congratulated you . . .'

'Oh, *that*—I thought you were being sarcastic, congratulating me on the smooth handling of a nasty situation with Ben.' He shrugged. 'I suppose I was feeling rather pleased seeing myself in the role of diplomat. As for marrying Morna, she's like a little sister to me, a girl I love and want to protect, but I assure you she doesn't arouse any of the emotions I would expect in the girl I marry . . .'

And I knew he was right. Nor could I blame Ben because he too had loved me like a brother and because his family had helped us spread our youthful illusion that it was something deeper. Ben—wise Ben, had known the difference the day he met Debbie.

'Morna is marrying Max Craig,' Fraser was saying. 'It's a long and complicated story. They fell in love on Max's first visit to Tillicross. Unfortunately he had married young and had been divorced for many years. Even if he hadn't been nearly twenty years older than Morna, her father belongs to a very strict religious sect who don't recognise divorce, so Mr. Keir wouldn't countenance any idea of marriage between them. Max only learned recently after lengthy enquiries that his first wife who had gone to Australia when she remarried, had in fact died there three years ago. Max has taken a new job in California and intends that Mr. Keir should live with them, as the climate would be better for him than Deveron. But he only managed to persuade Mr. Keir to give his consent the night we went to Tillicross for dinner. That was the reason Morna collected me in her car, to give the two men a chance to talk without her being present. Jeannie Deveron has always been very good to her, so she was the first to be told.'

'Did you know that Morna was at Tillicross when we were there that morning?'

'No—was she?'

'Yes, I saw her a couple of times, but obviously she didn't want to be seen.'

'She's still under the influence of a very strict and Puritanical upbringing, and marrying Max or no, her father would be shocked at the idea of them being alone together in the house. She must have been feeling very guilty, because she's always respected his beliefs no matter how severe. Why on earth didn't you mention seeing her?—no wonder Max was so eager to get rid of us. I could have taken the hint.'

'I was afraid she might turn out to be another of my apparitions at first. Then I thought when she didn't appear, perhaps you didn't know about Max and that she was being unfaithful.'

'So you wanted to protect me? Or did you think I might have a temper to go with the colour of my hair?'

'Something like that.'

'Which brings me to the next item on the agenda. Haven't you *any* idea who *I* am going to marry?'

I shook my head.

'Come here, you idiot,' he said softly. But there was nothing gentle about the kiss that followed. It was very thorough and aroused all those tumultuous sensations that came the first time, when we met the deer on the hillside. My heart was still beating wildly when he released me and said : 'Well, does that give you any clues as to who she might be?'

'Oh, Fraser . . .'

'Is that all you can say? Darling, I love you—I'm mad about you and I'd have told you that day in the hills, because sometimes I thought the feeling was mutual, that you liked me a little bit. You see I'd never had time to fall in love until you came along—and then you had to be engaged to someone else. I was in despair, I can tell you—wretched girl—I might never have found out that Ben was going to marry this American girl—it came out quite by accident when we were chatting in the caravan last night. Oh, I realise how hurt you must have been, but honestly, I was so glad I could have danced with joy. And then it seemed that you still wanted him,' he added despondently, 'so I had to let you go back with him and work it out for yourself. You needn't imagine for a moment that I was going to accept defeat so easily. I had it all planned to come down to York later this summer . . .'

'Oh, Fraser . . .'

He kissed me again. 'I'll be very patient and not rush you. I just wanted you to know that I love you in case we discover your secret room and then you might think it was just out of gratitude because we had found the Allan Ramsay portrait.'

'Before we go, kiss me again, please.' That took rather a long time and when Fraser released me, and the library bounded back to the perspective where it belonged, I said :

'I do love you . . .'

'Shh. Don't protest too much. I'm not greedy and years of wrestling with Deveron have taught me all about being patient. I can wait for what I want—just love me a little, the rest will come.'

He put his arm around me and we walked across the Great Hall down the corridor where our search would begin. For a little while it seemed that my hunch had been wrong, for he couldn't remember a white rose among the heraldic patterns on the stained-glass windows. Then at last we found it, with such ease that it seemed our search was over.

Except that in the panel facing us there was no door, just solid wood.

'I'm sure this is the place,' I said.

Fraser looked at the rose and sighed. 'You could be wrong. There might be half a dozen glass panes exactly like this. Let's keep on looking.'

But there was only one white rose and we were back looking at the solid wood, trying some means of locating what had been a hidden door in my nocturnal adventure.

Minutes passed while Fraser tested every place that might conceal a spring. Finally he leaned back and said : 'I give up.'

'I'm so sorry. I must have been wrong. I must have dreamed the whole thing.'

'Cheer up, darling. There's one way to find out, isn't there?'

He disappeared downstairs and returned with some tools. As he worked I watched anxiously. What if I had built up his hopes, only to dash them? What if it had been only a vivid dream or some kind of time-travel? Standing by helplessly, I lived over a hundred times the moment of discovery of what lay behind that panel—nothing but empty space, the cobwebs of centuries.

'Here goes. Keep your fingers crossed.' There was a rending of wood as the door crashed inward. Holding up his torch, Fraser shone it into the dark cobwebs I had already decided would meet our eyes. I could hardly speak for disappointment, I felt the tears welling, overflowing : 'Oh, Fraser,' I wailed, 'it wasn't like this at all ! It's the wrong place.'

Fraser had pushed aside the cobwebs, shone the torch into the dark interior. 'But by heaven, it isn't !' he shouted triumphantly. 'There is something in there. Look.'

Inside was a small glimmer of light, from a long

narrow slit of window. Then in the darkness eyes gleamed in the torch's beam, eyes from a life-size portrait of a girl holding a white rose.

We scrambled through the place where the panel had been and Fraser excitedly examined the picture. It seemed ages before he said anything as he looked at it minutely, his face solemn. So long that I wondered once again, had it all been useless—was he going to tell me that this was only a copy, that his grandmother had been cleverer than he thought and sold the original?

'Is it—is it . . . ?'

Slowly he turned, nodded. 'Yes, it's undoubtedly the Allan Ramsay. My darling, do you realise what this means? Not only will we keep a roof on Devron but we'll put it to the use I have always intended. Castles were built for people, not as grand mausoleums packed with priceless antiques and lovely furniture, roped off to be admired with twenty-five pence per head. We only need a fraction of it for ourselves, the rest I'm going to turn into an hotel for handicapped people—adults, children who would never otherwise have a holiday. I'll put in lifts and all the gadgets I've devised and improvised in the Glasgow flats.'

He put his arm around me, held me close to his side. 'Take a good look at the White Rose. Now that I've seen her I don't even want to keep her here—she too belongs where she can be seen and admired by many. And by selling her we give her to the world. Instead of the one man she gave her life trying to save— the man born to be king, now she'll live again, buy new hope and happiness for many. I think she would want that, don't you?'

As he spoke, the torchlight wavered on the canvas and for a moment it seemed that she smiled on us.

'Is the room exactly as you remembered it?'

'Yes. Even to the bed with its cobwebbed curtains.'

'See that dint on the pillow? That was probably made by Prince Charles when he slept hidden here after Culloden. I wonder how many more secrets this room has in store for us?' A careful search of the trunk I had seen revealed nothing but a collection of family papers. Gathering them together and closing the lid, Fraser sat back on his heels and said:

'There's one thing wrong with your story, Candida. Nobody ever took the White Rose portrait through a solid wall. And as for you, my love, you're quite beautiful but not in the least ethereal—how then did you manage to travel through a door that doesn't exist and who replaced—and repaired the cobwebs after your departure? You couldn't have walked through that gossamer veil without destroying it.'

The torch's beam raked the floor. 'Look—notice anything peculiar?'

'There are only two sets of footprints in the dust.'

'Correct. And they are ours. Which means you neither walked on the floor nor disturbed the centuries old cobwebs when you were here before. How did you manage it?'

'I don't know, but I imagine it was in the same way I walked down a dangerous mountainside the day I got lost on Cairn Dever. I seemed to walk through a tunnel of mist.' I went over to the corner cupboard, opened it, and there was the concealed door which led out on to the spiral stairs. 'There are some of your answers. That's how the picture was transported and that is the way I escaped from this room.'

I turned to him smiling. Suddenly he took hold of me, held me close with my face pressed hard against his shoulder. 'Let's go,' he whispered, 'before I start seeing things.'

'What's wrong?' I thought he looked pale and strange.

'Nothing. Just let us go . . .'

And long afterwards he told me that as I stood at the door in the torchlight I was someone else. The White Rose and Candida Deveron Brent, were, for an instant in time, one and the same person.